Fugue

The Amnesia Love Story That Will Make You Forget Every Other Amnesia Love Story

Mickey Hadick

PARKSIDE BOOKS
HOLT, MICHIGAN

Copyright © 2017 Mickey Hadick; All Rights Reserved.
No part of this document may be reproduced or transmitted in any form or by any means without prior permission of Mickey Hadick.

Disclaimers
This is a work of fiction. All characters and events are the product of the author's imagination. Any resemblance to characters, living or dead, is coincidental.

ISBN-13: 978-1541209268
Library of Congress Control Number: 2017919142
Date of publication: December 2017

Cover graphics by Michael Reibsome
Interior design by Mickey Hadick

Published by Parkside Books
Holt, Michigan
www.ParksideBooks.net

Farmer Hoggett knew that little ideas that tickled and nagged and refused to go away should never be ignored, for in them lie the seeds of destiny.

Babe, 1995

Other books by Mickey Hadick:

Fiction:

Ten Stories
Sally and Billy in Babyland, and Their Adventures With Kitty the Cat

Non-Fiction:

Ignite Your Life
Boss Lessons
The Daily Fitness Secret

Sign up for updates and deals on books at:

www.mickeyhadick.com

Fugue

The Amnesia Love Story That Will Make You Forget Every Other Amnesia Love Story

Mickey Hadick

CHAPTER ONE

Lina Finnerty realized that her marriage was ending, right there on the altar, before it started. If there were no more commotion they might get through the ceremony. But was this how to start a happily-ever-after?

Just as the pastor cleared his throat to begin, Lina took one last glance over her shoulder at her ex-boyfriend, Harold. But Harold wasn't looking back at Lina as she expected. Harold stared gape-mouthed at the woman across the aisle flashing a boob.

"Son of a bitch." Lina watched with disbelief as the woman worked to fit the boob back into the too-small top. And what a boob it was, big enough that if you tattooed "Goodyear" on the side there would still be space for a picture of an all-season, radial tire.

She heard laughter. Right there next to her on the altar, Joe, her groom, snickering.

Index-middle-ring-pinkie, Lina counted as she touched her thumb against each finger on her right hand. *Index-middle-ring-pinkie*, allowing the tic to repeat as she breathed deeply to self-soothe.

Brittney, her maid of honor, offered a soft touch on Lina's shoulder. "I bet it's the strippers from the bachelor party."

Every wedding guest had by now turned in their pew to see the stripper, a red-head with dark eyes, along with her stacked, frizzy-blonde of a friend, step into the aisle and sashay out of the church.

Joe struggled to wipe the smirk off his face.

Index-middle-ring-pinkie, she tapped with her thumb. "What in the name of God have you done?" Lina hissed, realizing too late that she had used one of her mother's catch-phrases.

Until that moment, Lina believed her marriage would last. She wasn't getting married because she had to. And she wasn't checking off one more thing on her life-to-do-list—college, MBA, and marriage. She thought this was the guy for her.

But here they were, not even married, and she had to deal with betrayal.

"I didn't invite her," Joe said.

"You should go tip her," Gary, the best man, said, laughing even before he finished.

Lina bounced the bouquet off of his child-like face.

Index-middle-ring-pinkie, she tapped. "It's not funny."

"It's not meant to be funny," Joe said. "But it *is* funny. I mean, come on—"

"Shut up." Again, the angry bark reminded herself of her mother, Pauline.

Pauline sat front and center, right on the aisle, glaring up at the altar, gripping the edge of the pew, hunched forward as if ready to spring out and attack. They'd fought like dogs over the guests, the dress, the decorations, the reception and now, well, none of it mattered as it all had gone in the shitter.

The people Pauline insisted that Lina had to invite were all there, all of them beautiful, dressed in fine clothes, lovely hair, and tan skin. These were the people Pauline had met since they left the west side after the ugly divorce and somehow forced their way into the east side's society, courtesy of the orthodontist Pauline had married.

The jewelry sparkled on both men and women. But those lovely people now stared up at Lina like they'd discovered the gardener dead in the back yard and worried who would clean up the mess.

Across the aisle were Joe's guests, a mixed bag of Walmart shoppers and sports fans. You had to admit, they dressed comfortably. Several of them craned their necks to see if a fight might yet break out.

Harold was the only one with a sympathetic look on his face. Taller than most, his bright eyes sparkled in a ray of light through the stained glass windows. She hadn't invited him, so how did he even know about the wedding?

And why had Joe not done something about the strippers sooner? He must have seen them come in. Why didn't he send Gary to pay them and cast them out?

No. Her mind was still clear on the subject. This was not just one incident but instead an epiphany that explained a feeling she'd struggled to admit. Now it was clear.

She was ashamed.

Lina looked at Joe. How could he let this happen?

Joe shrugged.

How could you *marry* someone who shrugs?

Lina tapped, *index-middle-ring-pinkie, index-middle-ring-pinkie...*

Joe smiled. "At least it can't get any worse."

Gary chuckled.

"Are you trying to make a joke?" Lina asked.

"He jokes," Brittney said, "but he's not funny."

"Oh what do you know about funny?" Joe asked.

Brittney stepped into his face. "I know how stupid you can be, you and your little toady of a friend."

"Hey—"

"Shut up," Lina said. "Shut up all of you."

Joe took Lina by the hand but she yanked it free again.

"Lina, come on," he said.

The roar erupted out of Lina's throat and—tearing at her lungs in its panic to escape—twisted and spun into a piercing scream that blocked out the mess she was in. It blocked out the pastor on the altar, the stripper leaving the church and her mother glaring from the pew.

What sort of wedding was this, anyway? Why bother searching the racks for an affordable gown that also suited her shoulders? Why go to *hot-yoga* three times a week, run 5Ks on the weekend, and lose ten pounds she didn't need to lose if this is how the big day turns out? Why get up early to have the stylist put your auburn hair in a tight bun and your beautician emphasize cheekbones and lips when the tears welling up in your eyes are all that people will remember? What's the point of planning for twelve months and sweating the decorations if all you do is invite your friends and family to a total fiasco?

Lina realized the roar from her throat had subsided when she inhaled to catch her breath.

The guests stared at her like she was a circus freak show—and who could blame them? She'd done everything possible to be gorgeous but, instead, she turned into a monster, the sort of control freak she'd promised herself she'd never be. And Joe, the master of Zen who was supposed to help her learn to be chill had, instead, pushed her into becoming exactly the thing she hated most—her wrathful mother.

"They're gone," Joe said. "Let's get married before a virgin, shepherd, and two sheep come out for the next act."

Lina felt her brow constrict as she looked at him. Was this the man she was marrying?

"Whoa," Joe said. "Tough crowd."

Lina stepped down from the altar.

Carl, her would-be father-in-law, stepped out of the pew before her. "Lina, please. Don't do this to Joe. He's a fool but he loves you."

Michael, her step-father, stepped out of the pew across the aisle and grabbed Carl by the shoulder. "You shut the hell up." They locked onto each other, pushing back and forth like overgrown children wrestling in tuxedos.

Carl's thick face and neck turned red, and Michael's tan skin glistened with sweat as the struggle turned them into grotesques.

Lina tried to step past but they blocked the aisle, now more like angry penguins fighting over a dead fish.

The guests stood in their pews and surged toward the center. In another moment they would pour out into the aisle, blocking her escape.

Pauline stumbled into the pew as she shoved at them, yelling, "You fools."

They lurched back to the other side of the aisle, leaving a path down the aisle to the back of the church.

Lina wanted to be alone. She wanted to be away from the idiots gathered here today on her behalf. And Lina did not want to deal with her mother.

Index-middle-ring-pinkie. Breathe. Find a place to breathe and think.

So she ran.

Lina focused on the church door at the other end of the aisle, blocking out the chaos, concentrating on what she could control—her feet moving as quickly as possible.

But her foot caught on something and she lurched forward, airborne, pitching head first along the pews. Like her wedding, her escape was ending before it started. She made eye contact with her mother on the way down. It must have been the adrenaline but Lina saw the angry set of her mother's eyebrows, the flared nostrils and how her mouth clenched shut.

The side of the pew swept past as she turned her face away from the fast approaching tile floor.

She closed her eyes.

CHAPTER TWO

Joe froze where he stood. Not only had he pissed off Lina, but now she looked dead.

The first guy to Lina was Harold, the ex-boyfriend, who dropped to his knees and checked Lina's vital signs.

"I've already called an ambulance," Harold said.

"What are you even doing here?" Joe asked.

Harold produced a pen light and looked inside Lina's mouth, then peeled back her eyelids. "It's a good thing I'm here."

Pauline shoved her way past Joe. "What have you done to my daughter?"

Then Michael, the step-father, grabbed Joe by the shoulder and flung him back to the altar.

The pastor helped Joe to his feet but said nothing. There was no scripture in the good book for this situation.

People swarmed around Lina. Joe pressed into the crowd but he was grabbed and yanked aside. It was Michael again, glaring at Joe, the look in his eye threatening.

Carl intervened and Michael punched him, knocking Carl on his ass right there in the aisle.

Joe shoved Michael from behind. Michael launched a round-house that Joe ducked, but it caught Rhonda, Joe's sister, right on the nose. She was bleeding like a stuck pig before her ass had settled on the ground.

"What the hell is your problem?" Joe shouted at Michael.

Michael took a breath as if to say something, but lashed out with his left and followed with a right, ringing Joe's bell and dropping him in the aisle next to the rest of his family.

It stung like crazy. Joe laid back, holding his face where it hurt. There was a painting on the ceiling, of all places, some corn-ball clouds and two angels with Jesus, his arms out and palms showing with a *what-me-worry?* grin on his face.

Joe sat up in front of the altar and offered Rhonda his kerchief.

"If you didn't want to get married," Rhonda asked, "you could have just said so."

"What are you talking about?" Joe said. "Of course I want to get married."

"Why the hell did you invite strippers?"

"I didn't invite them. And I will marry Lina."

Rhonda pointed. "You'd better stay by your bride," she said. "The ambulance is here."

It was true. The paramedics were already checking on Lina.

The wedding guests had blocked the aisle even tighter and Joe realized it would be faster out the side door and back in the front door.

But Gary stopped Joe in the Family Room where they had gotten ready before the ceremony. "Hold up, man." Gary offered Joe the bottle of whiskey.

"Can't you do something helpful? You're the Best Man."

Gary tipped the bottle to his mouth for another gulp. "I'm the best you got."

The pastor approached Joe. "There is the matter of the payment."

"But you didn't even marry us."

The pastor shrugged. "Sins can be forgiven but debts must still be paid."

"Pastor, please. I'm not even sure where my wallet is."

"I have faith in you," the pastor said as he stepped into the doorway, blocking Joe's path. "But given the circumstances, I must insist on cash."

Joe went back into the church where he found his father helping Rhonda towards the nave. "I need money," he said. "It's for the church."

"I'm not giving you another penny," Carl said.

Joe stooped down to make eye contact with Rhonda as she held a towel to her nose. "How about you, Sis? Do you have a couple hundred?"

"How were you going to pay him?"

"I have no idea. Lina was handling all the details."

"Too bad you didn't wait until the reception to ruin everything," Rhonda said. "There's probably a couple of thousand in cash with your name on it."

"Oh shut up."

"You shut up."

Joe looked out the front door. The paramedics were preparing to lift Lina into the ambulance. "Tell the pastor I'll owe it him." Joe turned and ran.

When he got to the front doors, Joe still had to zig-zag through the crowd. But he got to the ambulance before they lifted Lina's gurney.

"Lina, I'm so sorry," Joe said as he took hold of her hand.

Lina looked at him but said nothing.

"Please forgive me."

Lina seemed confused. "Forgive you for what?"

Joe felt a rush of joy and hopefulness. "Lina, baby, I am so glad you're not angry."

Lina pulled her hand away. "What are you talking about?"

Joe pointed with his thumb back at the church. "That little thing back there."

"Excuse me?"

Pauline stuck her face in front of Lina's. "Do you know who I am?"

"You're my mother."

Pauline pointed at Joe. "What about him? Do you know who he is?"

Lina blinked. "I've never seen him before in my life."

CHAPTER THREE

As they rolled into the examination area, Lina felt fine. It was like waking up from a dream but not quite remembering the dream.

"Where are we?" she asked.

"The hospital," Pauline said.

"Why are we here?"

"Please be quiet until the doctor has looked you over."

"Why are you so angry?" Lina asked.

"Because he ruined our wedding."

"What wedding?"

"Our wedding, dear," Pauline said and patted Lina's hand.

The nurse strapped a blood pressure cuff on Lina's arm and nodded as she took her pulse. "Was it the groom or the best man?" she asked.

"Both of them," Pauline said.

The nurse folded her arms. "I'll never marry again," she said. "What I need can be found easily enough."

As the nurse stepped out of the examination area, Lina gripped her mother's hand. "What the hell is she talking about?"

"There's no shame in it, Lina. Men have treated women like this many times before. This won't be the last. For women like us, the caring, trusting kind, our lives can be just one bad experience after another. Life is just a festival of wrongs and misdeeds."

"My God, mother—"

"Oh don't worry about me." Pauline leaned in close to Lina's ear. "I don't trust your step-father any more than I trusted your bio-father. But we have a nice house, don't we?"

Lina sat up in the bed. "Why are you telling me this?"

Harold, sporting a white lab coat over his shirt and tie, swept into the examination area.

"How are we doing?" he asked.

Joe's car – a dirty, rusted, 1979 Dodge Dart – pulled into a parking spot marked "Doctors Only" but Joe didn't care.

The Emergency Room reception area was just inside the door. There he found Michael, the would-be step-father-in-law, blocking Joe's path.

"You've done enough damage for one day," Michael asked.

Joe side stepped Michael. "I need to apologize."

Michael grabbed Joe by the arm and kept him out. "Leave now and I won't have to hurt you."

The nurse at the triage desk came into the waiting area. "What's going on?" she asked.

Michael squeezed Joe's shoulder hard. "This is the one I told you about."

The nurse nodded, sizing Joe up. "Family only," she said.

Joe smiled. "But I'm her husband."

The nurse shook her head. "I've called security."

FUGUE

Joe waited outside of the hospital. A few paces away, on the edge of the parking lot, was a smoking station—a glass box—where a few orderlies and nurses puffed away at cigarettes. If an ambulance arrived he could sneak in during the chaos. But there's never a gruesome car accident when you need one.

The folks in the smoking station were chatting and puffing. An older man pushed an old woman in a wheel chair towards the parking lot.

The nurse who chased him out of the Emergency Room strolled out of the hospital and busied herself lighting a cigarette as she made her way to the smoking station. She sat at one end, facing away from the hospital, and inhaled. She leaned back, watching the smoke gather at the glass roof.

Her bad habit was Joe's first lucky break of the day.

Joe marched back into the hospital but, avoiding the Emergency Room, walked like he knew what he was doing into the bowels of the place, pacing himself to fall in step with orderlies opening doors until he made his way to the nurse's station for the Emergency Room.

"Excuse me," Joe said. "I got turned around. Can you direct me to Lina Finnerty? She's the one in the bridal gown."

The nurse checked her computer. "Are you family?"

Joe tugged on the lapels of his jacket. "Almost. I was in the wedding party."

"Oh."

Joe grimaced. "Yeah, it was kind of crazy."

"She'll be back in station number three," the nurse said and pointed over her shoulder at the row of curtained areas. "But you have to wait in the lobby."

13

"No problem."

Lina's lower back ached. She hadn't moved a muscle except to hold an ice pack on her head. If only her mother would take a break, it might all be bearable.

"I'm thinking we keep the gifts that people already gave you," Pauline said. "Especially the cash."

"Jesus, mother. Give it a rest."

Harold slipped in between the curtains and waved an x-ray and a stack of papers over the bed. "I have good news and bad news."

"Oh good grief," Pauline said. "Tell us some good news."

"You have a concussion."

Pauline gripped the side rails on the bed and shook them. "That's the good news? What about the amnesia? Is it permanent?'

Lina sat up. "What amnesia?"

"You see? It's gotten worse. She doesn't even remember that she has amnesia."

Lina reached for Harold's arm. "What is she talking about?"

Harold waved his hand. "It's fine. It'll pass."

"But you said the concussion was the good news."

"Yes," Harold said. "It's mild. A smidgen of cranial bleeding."

"Lovely."

"But you don't remember who gave you this cranial bleeding, do you?" her mother asked.

"Was I attacked?"

"Your groom bushwhacked you."

"What does that even mean?"

FUGUE

"Joe surprised you by revealing his true self. And not a moment too soon, I might add."

"Wait, did you say 'groom'?"

Pauline lifted the bed covers, revealing the wedding dress.

"I was getting married?"

"Yes," Harold said. "You were beautiful."

Lina looked at Harold, then her mother. She must have prepped like hell for the wedding, how could she not —

"It's true, you looked beautiful. In spite of the trained monkey you'd chosen to join you in holy matrimony. It's no surprise he made a mockery of the entire thing."

"But it didn't happen?"

"Thank heavens, no," Pauline said. "You take after me when it comes to choosing your first husband. I hope you do better with the second choice."

"Harold was first."

Pauline looked at Harold. "Since you don't remember the other one, then this one is still a candidate."

Joe didn't bother with the slippers. He wore the shiny shoes from the tuxedo shop and they were the prettiest things he'd ever put on his feet. Otherwise, he covered his tuxedo with hospital scrubs.

With the cap on his head and the mask over his face, he kind of felt like a doctor. They were all frauds, anyway, so why not him?

Joe retraced his steps through the hallways. The nurse at the station in the Emergency Room was didn't look up from her smart phone.

Joe's pace slowed as he approached Examination Area #3. "And how is the patient?" he asked as he swept open the curtain. "Is that knock on the noggin' still stirring the noodles?"

They stared at him like he had golf balls for eyes.

"Excuse me?" Harold asked.

"May I see the chart?" Joe asked and took hold of the clipboard in Harold's hand.

But Harold didn't let go.

"I'd like to see her vitals, if you know what I mean."

Pauline stepped closer and pulled the surgical mask down from Joe's face.

"Hi," Joe said. "How's it hangin'?"

Pauline shook her head. "This is the irreverent, disrespectful, and inappropriate—"

"I want to see how my darling bride is doing."

"Excuse me?" Lina said.

Harold patted Lina's hand. "Lina, this is Joe, the groom."

"For real?" she asked.

What sort of pretentious, elitist crap was that? "I'm the guy who doesn't need an introduction."

Lina shook her head. "I don't remember you."

"Quit kiddin'," he said.

"She doesn't remember you, dumb-dumb," Pauline said. "You gave her amnesia when you shoved her."

"I didn't shove her."

"You may as well have. You chased her from the altar like she was a dog and then you stood there when she fell."

"I didn't know what—" Joe turned to Lina and said, "You—I love you and you have to remember me."

"I'm calling security," Pauline said.

FUGUE

"Wait," Lina said. "I have to ask…"

"What is it?" Harold asked.

Lina looked at Harold. "My first boyfriend, is a doctor, right?"

"Specialist," Harold said.

"And the guy I was going to marry is a doctor, right? So do I have a thing for doctors?"

The mean nurse trailed behind as the security guard escorted Joe out of the hospital.

"I don't want to see you back here unless you're on a stretcher," the nurse said. "And the scrubs are not yours."

Joe peeled off the scrubs. "She'll remember me, right?"

The nurse shrugged.

Harold approached. In the lab coat, shirt and tie, he looked like he knew what he was doing. Joe looked at his own messed up outfit—the loose shirt and tie, suspenders half off. It was his look.

"I'd like to help," Harold said. "If you'll indulge me."

"I'll talk to a proctologist if it'll help get my head out of my ass."

Harold nodded, his face suspicious. "You understand she has a concussion?"

"She gets better, what, in two days?"

"There may be complications of headaches or persistent nausea but in a day or two she'll heal."

"Then she remembers me?"

Harold shook his head. "That is far more complicated. I believe she is suffering a dissociative fugue because of transient amnesia."

"Say what?"

17

"Concussions disrupt short-term memory, leading to limited amnesia. It rarely effects long-term memories."

"Um, okay."

"But the dissociative fugue is psychological. I believe the stress of the wedding and the events during the wedding triggered a subconscious response."

"Come again?"

"She was traumatized and embarrassed. Then she suffered even more trauma by hitting her head. So her subconscious protected her psyche by removing the source of the trauma."

"The source of the trauma? But— but that's..."

"That's you. She's protecting herself by erasing you from her memory."

CHAPTER FOUR

Joe entered the hall and sat at the first table he approached. He was exhausted, and wanted to sleep more than anything. Another reason why drinking shots of Jack in the morning is rarely a good idea.

V.F.W. Post 2133 was a short, squat building with a few windows along one wall. At one end was a kitchen, accessible through a service counter. There was also a bar, toilets, and a storage room next to that. All the rest was open space.

Tables with chairs were set up for a meal. A banner on the wall proclaimed "Congratulations!" Streamers crisscrossed between the hanging light fixtures. Modest flower arrangements marked the center of each table. Lina had been incredibly busy the past year, literally working hard enough for both of them, leaving the decorations to Rhonda and Brittney.

"Come on, man," Gary, surrounded by friends and fools they met at school, shouted to Joe from the bar. "Shots."

Why shouldn't he? These guys were here for him—or because of free food and booze—but still a little for him. Everyone was there for the food and booze. At least Gary called for him.

Joe got up and made his way across the hall but his sister stopped him.

"What are you doing?" she asked. She sounded weird with her nose plugged and bandaged. She looked like you'd think someone would look after being punched in the nose.

"I'm going to drink with my friends. You know, those people that like you no matter what. Of which you have none."

"Fuck off."

"What is the problem?"

"For starters, the caterer wants to know what to do with the food. I told her to feed anybody and everybody and donate the rest, if that's okay."

"I don't care." Joe stepped past her but she grabbed his suspenders.

"What are you doing to fix this?"

"Get drunk."

"Moron," she said. "That's what caused the problem."

Gary brought Joe a drink. "Shots, man."

Rhonda shook her head. "Team moron."

"Big nose," Gary said.

"Fix this tonight."

"Lina has amnesia," Joe said. "She doesn't know who I am.."

Rhonda's anger waned. "I'm sorry. That sucks. What did the doctor say?"

"You mean her boyfriend."

"Crud, that's right. You really do have to fix this right now."

Joe shrugged. Rhonda was crazy. There was nothing to do but drink. He'd get arrested if he returned to the hospital. If that wasn't a reason to drink with his friends then he'd have to get drunk for no reason.

Rhonda wouldn't let it go, and pulled their father into the discussion.

"I say we kick his ass," Carl said.

"Who?"

"That son of a bitch father-in-law of yours. I'll kick his ass."

"Dad, no," Rhonda said.

"He better pay for your nose job."

Joe motioned for another shot. "He didn't like me before. This won't help."

Rhonda spilled out the shot before Joe could throw it down. "You need to fix this."

"What do you care?"

"I like Lina."

"Well, shit, I was going to marry her."

"Yeah," Rhonda said, "and I would have a family member I like."

"The feeling is mutual."

"She is smart, fashionable, sensible, and engaging."

"Relax."

Rhonda was riled up. "Lina had a full ride to Case Western. John Carroll gave her even more to get her M.B.A. She was talking about law school."

Okay," Joe said. "This is not making me feel better."

"What the hell were you thinking, asking those girls to the wedding."

"Don't look at me," Gary said. "I only asked for a blow job."

"I don't remember doing even that," Joe said.

"It's like you have stripper amnesia," Gary said.

Rhonda punched Joe in the arm. "Why the hell didn't you get them out of church?"

"I tried."

Rhonda threw a glass of water in Joe's face. "No you didn't."

"God damn stuck-up East-siders," Gary said as he stuffed sauerkraut into his mouth.

Rhonda had sat them down at a table with food. "There must be something you can do. And she won't even be at the hospital. They would send her home to rest."

"Why do you even care?" Joe asked as he cut into his kielbasa.

"I lost my mother when I was nine. Lina is the best thing ever. I deserve a decent family, God damn it."

Joe shrugged. "Okay, sorry I ruined your life again. But her family hates me more than ever."

"Pauline won't leave her alone. You need to visit her over there, at Pauline's house."

Gary poured another shot for Joe but Rhonda swept it aside.

"Hey—"

Rhonda threw a glass of water in Gary's face. "You need to help, okay? This is serious."

Gary rubbed an eye. "What the hell?"

"You get him to Pauline's house and help Joe find Lina."

"What then?" Joe asked.

Rhonda snapped her finger in Joe's face. "Charm them. Kiss ass. Whatever it takes to get near Lina. If she sees you in a pleasant setting, she may remember you sooner. And

FUGUE

if she never remembers you, maybe she'll like you anyway."

"Sounds like a long shot," Joe said.

Rhonda stuck a fork into a potato pierogi. "Win her back before she remembers that there are still a few fish left in Lake Erie."

CHAPTER FIVE

Lina cried. She wasn't sure, exactly, what made her cry but there seemed a litany of topics. No need to pick just one.

A nurse—a nice nurse, not like the one that dragged what's-his-name away—brought her yet another blanket. "For what it's worth," she said, "I thought he was charming."

Pauline scoffed. "Yes they all are—at first."

"I just meant—"

"Yes thank you. Your insight has been very helpful."

The nice nurse snatched the water bottle from the tray. "I'll go get ice."

"She was being nice," Lina hissed.

"Only fools are nice without a good reason, and I don't have time for fools."

Harold entered the examination area. "Good news," he said. "A colleague agrees that the concussion's minor."

"Thank heaven," Pauline said. "Can we leave?"

"Yes. Rest and observation is all you need."

Pauline grabbed her own purse and peeled back a layer of blankets from Lina. "Then let's go before something else happens."

Lina grabbed her mother's wrist. "What about the amnesia?"

"That will have to run its course," Harold said.

"But how long?"

"Oh sweetheart," her mother said. "You'll rest, and then you'll move on with your life."

Lina pulled the blanket back up over her wedding dress and tapped the fingers of her right hand with her thumb, *index-middle-ring-pinkie.*

With a cold shudder of dread, Lina remembered her mother's house without flaw. The kitchen was an open layout with stainless steel appliances and granite countertops, the cliched presentation of would-be well-to-dos, as if her mother flipped through one issue of Architectural Digest and three Home and Garden magazines, and then ordered up her kitchen to match the pictures.

This so-called fugue was baffling—she wasn't struggling to remember what she remembered. She remembered her mother, and her stepfather, and even Harold.

"Do you remember your room upstairs?"

"Yes."

"Do you remember Joe?"

"No."

"Good," Pauline said. "I hate that son of a bitch."

Lina stopped and faced her mother. "I also remember your hatred. That seems to be the sharpest memory of all."

"What do you mean?"

Lina tapped the fingers on her right hand with her thumb, *index-middle-ring-pinkie.* "Your hatred. The unhappiness. It's always been there and I don't like it."

"Well you've told me plenty of things you don't like about me," Pauline said. "Forgive me if I slip up every once in a while."

Lina left it alone. She didn't need her doctor to tell her that rest was more important than winning a battle with her mother.

And luckily she didn't need her former boyfriend to step in and help with the argument, because apparently all that Harold wanted to do was fall into step behind her like a dog.

Harold carried the train of the wedding dress upstairs. "I don't remember this. Was I here?"

"Yes. Like four years ago."

"Really?"

"We spent an entire weekend here my freshman year while my mother and Michael were on a cruise."

"I guess I remember that."

"Thanks."

Her room was like it had been in high school. Even when Lina made changes during these past few years at college, her mother had changed it back so that the posters and equestrian ribbons were on the wall, gymnastics trophies on the shelf, and stuffed animals on the bed.

Lina moved about the room, brushing against things in her dress. "Why am I here, in this room, in this dress?"

Joe and Gary were parked on the street a house and a half down from Pauline's house.

"You going in?" Gary asked.

"I want to wait until Dr. Smarty-pants leaves."

"Don't be a pussy," Gary said. He reached into the back seat and grabbed two beers. "Maybe if you're a little more drunk you'll punch him in the face instead of waiting until he's done banging your wife."

FUGUE

#

When Joe was four, Lina lived just around the corner. The houses on the street were all tiny, two-bedroom homes built in the 50s. Maybe the awnings were different, or the color of the roof. Some houses were brick, others with clapboard or aluminum siding.

They were all on square chunks of yard with a driveway running from the street, past the house and into the back yard. Some had a garage in back but there were always cars parked on the street.

At the end of the road, where their little brick road ran into a bigger road, was a hamburger shop. You couldn't even eat at the place—no tables or chairs—just a window to place your order. So every day in summer, Joe and Lina walked with Lina's mom to get a hamburger.

When you're four, you think every other four-year old thinks the same as you do, and wants the same things you want.

And you think all the moms and dads are just like your own mom and dad. They just had different kids and lived in a different house. But they were all moms and dads with kids. They were all families just like your own.

You don't realize that things are different.

It was always Lina's mom who took them because that was when Joe's mom first got sick, and she was in bed a lot. Joe thought Lina's mom understood that about his mom.

Joe's mom gave him a dollar and a quarter, which was enough money to buy a hamburger, a shake, and fries.

They would walk back to Lina's house and ate at her kitchen table, spreading out the hamburger wrappers. Joe liked to dip his fries in his milkshake. Lina arranged and ate her fries in order of their length, smallest to the largest.

One day, Lina's mom said, "Does your mother ever leave the house?"

"Not when she's sick," Joe said.

"Does she drink in the morning, and then get sick?"

"No," Joe said. "She wakes up sick."

"Oh," Lina's mom said. "A hangover."

Joe didn't know what she meant but he knew she was angry about it. That was the first time he realized that maybe Lina's mom was not like his own mom.

# # #

Lina sat on the edge of her childhood bed and clutched her favorite toy, a plush, pink unicorn named "Marcie." Lina was wearing her mother's robe and pulled Marcie the unicorn close, stroking its rainbow mane. Marcie had been Lina's best friend through the years. When things were tough, like often in sixth grade, when girls can be mean, and more often in eighth grade, when the mean girls get good at being mean, and almost all the time through high school, when things seemed confusing even if no one was mean about it. Marcie had been through it all. Since Marcie was here, at her mother's house, and this thing happened to her head, maybe Lina had better keep Marcie the unicorn nearby to help her remember.

FUGUE

In fact, Lina seemed to remember something about her room already. "We had sex here, right?" she asked. "In this bed?"

"Yes," Harold said. He leaned against the door frame and shifted his weight. "At least once."

"I thought so." If she remembered but he didn't, then her brain might be inventing things. "There was that weekend thing, and once during a picnic out back. We snuck up here for a quickie."

"I believe—"

"They were all quickies for you, is that it?"

"I've practiced."

"You practiced?" Lina laughed. "Like with a doll?"

"What's so funny?"

"Are you embarrassed?"

"No. I saw a problem and I fixed it."

"Good for you."

Harold approached the bed. "Mind if I take one last look?"

"You mean my boobs?"

"No. Your ability to focus." He removed a pen light from his pocket and waved it in front of her face. "Besides, I have pictures of your boobs. Don't you remember?"

Lina positioned Marcie the unicorn across her chest. "No I don't."

"Good, because nothing like that happened." Harold returned to the safety of the doorway.

"Well?"

"You're ability to track is fine. How's the head?"

Lina put a hand to the bump. "Still hurts."

"Okay, then rest is still the prescription. I'll have your mother check on you throughout the night."

"Is that necessary?"

"No but I'd like to mess with her."

Lina motioned for Harold to wait. She looked him over, trying to figure out what he meant by practicing. "Do you hire prostitutes?"

Harold shook his head. "Are you sure you're not dizzy?"

"You can't handle a simple question without wondering if I'm crazy?"

"That's not a simple question. It's unusual."

"How do you practice?"

Harold backed closer to the door. "I don't think I'll tell you."

The Mercedes backed out of the driveway and Gary reached across the seat and took away Joe's beer.

"It's time," Gary said.

"I know, I know."

"Don't be a pussy."

"Screw you."

"Pussy."

Joe got out of the car. With a friend like Gary, who needed an enema.

The houses sat far back off of the street. It was a once-prestigious neighborhood, if you believed what Pauline told you, and had been posh and impressive during the fifties. Most were brick, a few of them in fieldstone, and the rest were wood siding. There was no aluminum siding like the houses back in his own neighborhood.

Shrubs and flowers decorated the front lawns. Cement statues of jockeys and horses stood near front garden paths. And the windows in most homes featured signs about the neighborhood watch or ADT security. Joe felt unwelcome.

But back in Parma, where Joe felt at ease, pink flamingos stared at each other in pairs on the tiny front lawns.

Pauline's house was a Tudor with brick and stucco exterior. There was a tall, steep gable over the front door, and the window to Lina's room was up there, near that peak. The light was still on.

Joe knocked on the front door.

Heavy steps approached.

Michael opened the door. "What? You?" Michael charged at him, chasing Joe off the steps and across the lawn.

"Hey, come on, I wanted—"

"Whatever you want, the answer is no."

"Well, what if I *don't* want to see Lina? Would you *make* me?"

Michael returned to the front door and paused a moment to glare at Joe before shutting and locking the door.

"Fuck you," Joe said, but not so loud that Michael heard him.

# # #

Preschool started at the end of summer. Lina knocked on the side door every morning and waited for Joe to come outside.

Joe would be in the kitchen, eating cereal, anticipating the moment when Lina knocked on the door. That's what he liked about preschool—he got to see Lina.

Lina's mother waited on the sidewalk, smoking a cigarette as Lina and Joe walked down the driveway.

One morning it seemed about to rain. "Maybe we should drive," Joe said. "Don't you have a car?" He didn't mean anything by it. He thought they'd get wet if it rained.

"Does your mother have a car?" Lina's mother asked. "Because I sure don't. She's welcome to help out once in a while. Do you think she might want to do that?"

Joe shrugged. He didn't know why she was so mad.

Joe's mother had baby-Rhonda to deal with, and she did little around the house. Joe got himself a bowl of cereal when he woke up, picked out clothes, and his mother gave him spare change for lunch money. He never asked her to drive because he'd much rather walk with Lina.

They walked on the sidewalk along the red brick road, past house after house with different bushes and different awnings.

Lina liked to see how close to the edge she could get without touching the grass.

Joe liked to jump over the driveways, or sometimes he would trip on each crack in the sidewalk. If he did that, sometimes Lina would laugh, and then he'd do it more.

But sometimes Lina's mother would get mad because of Joe's goofing around, and then Lina would get mad.

And that morning when it seemed about to rain, she said, "Hurry or we will get caught in the rain."

"I'm sorry," Joe said.

"You're sorry but I have to walk back home after leaving you at school. Then I walk back again later to bring you home."

"Please, mom," Lina said.

Her mother smacked Lina's behind.

FUGUE

Joe stopped where he was but that made Lina's mother mad too.

"What's the matter with you?" she said. "Legs don't work? Do you want something to cry about?"

At school, they sat at the same table, and Lina would help him color. But that day, Lina wouldn't talk to Joe. She wouldn't help Joe with his coloring, or with his lettering, or anything.

"Are you okay?" Joe asked.

"Leave me alone," Lina said.

# # #

As a precautionary measure, Gary drove around the block and they approached Pauline's house from the other side.

"Sounds like you spent a lot of time with Lina's mom," Gary said.

Joe gazed at Lina's bedroom window. "I had no idea my mom was sick until she told me about a month before she died."

Gary parked in a dark area between two street lamps, a few more houses away than before. "That's messed up."

"She didn't do it on purpose. She just died."

The light in Lina's room switched off. "Try not to mess up this time," Gary said.

"What did you expect me to do."

"Nothing because you suck."

Joe got out of the car and started his approach. He stayed across the street and tried to walk casually, but at this late hour he didn't feel casual. If Michael was standing

33

guard, there'd be no way to avoid him. And now he was angry at what Gary said.

Joe crossed the street and cut across the yard at an angle, keeping watch on the first floor windows.

Joe moved the bird bath in the flower bed under the eave, using it as a step up. He got onto the steep roof of the front gable, and scraped and clawed his way to the main roof. He slipped twice, and dug his foot into the eaves trough to stay up, but he figured out how to climb the shingles.

Joe pushed on Lina's window. He tried to lift it but it wouldn't budge.

Joe tapped on the window. There was movement inside and the window opened.

"Lina, it's me—"

But it wasn't Lina. It was Michael, her step-father, who leaned out of the window.

Joe leaned back away to keep a certain distance. "Hello Mr. Sabbath."

Michael shook his head.

"I know this seems unusual but I had the best—"

Michael raised a finger as if to say something.

"Do you want to talk about this inside?"

Michael shook his head.

"Do you want me to leave now?"

Michael nodded.

"Oh. Well I guess—"

Then Michael shoved Joe off of the roof.

CHAPTER SIX

Lina stood up and pulled her step-father out of the way and looked out the window. "Did you kill him?"

"If we're lucky," Michael said.

Lina faced him and shook Marcie the unicorn in his face. "No. I'm not like that. I didn't think you were like that."

Pauline came in. "You need to rest and recover." She crossed to the window and pulled the shade closed. "Joe needs to think about what he has done."

Lina went to the window and looked out. Joe waved from the front lawn.

"He's upset. It's his wedding night."

"It's our wedding night too," Pauline said. "And he ruined it."

Lina hugged Marcie. "Ours?"

"Yes, 'ours.' Weddings are family events. I know you didn't want my help but you're my only daughter, so this was very important to me."

Lina set Marcie down. "It was my wedding mother. Mine."

Lina stepped past Michael and looked out the window. "The man you pushed off of the roof wanted to marry me."

"That guy doesn't deserve you," Michael said.

"That was my mistake to make."

Pauline scoffed. "You took advantage."

That tone was familiar. Her mother had used it during Lina's junior prom, when she went to the dance with a kid who was black. "You are unbelievable, mother. You never, ever seem to change."

"I'm trying to help you," Pauline said. "Don't you want my help?"

"I don't."

Pauline inhaled sharply, jutting out her chin. "You don't change either, young lady."

They sat on the porch steps of the colonial across the street, their view limited by an oak tree in the front yard.

"Do you think she'll remember me?" he asked.

"It doesn't matter," Gary said. He stood up from the front steps and walked back and forth across the lawn. "You need to punch that jerk step-father in the neck and kick him in the balls."

"I'm trying to join their family, not kill them off."

"How long have you been putting up with shit from Lina's parents?"

"Forever."

"Right. So what good is it doing us to sit here across the street?"

"They probably called the cops."

Gary shrugged.

"If I'm in jail I can't see Lina."

"You aren't seeing her now so what's the difference."

Joe stood up. Gary had a point—he needed to change how things were.

"About fucking time," Gary said.

FUGUE

Joe stepped onto the lawn, out of the shadows of the porch.

"Atta-boy," Gary said.

Across the street, Lina appeared on the front steps. She looked up and down the street.

Joe walked partway across the lawn.

"What are you waiting for?" Gary asked.

A police cruiser had turned the corner and drove along the street, picking up speed.

"What the fuck are you waiting for?"

Lina waved. It wasn't a beckoning wave—but she smiled.

Joe ran towards her, across the lawn and into the street.

The police cruiser hit its siren for a single, sour blast, drawing Joe's attention mid-stride, but too late to do anything to avoid contact.

Joe laughed. Being hit by a police car struck him as funny as he flipped over the hood. His face planted on the windshield and the cop's face appeared to Joe like a snapshot.

Time slowed as he rose up above the hood. A woman walking a small, white dog on the sidewalk in front of the next house over, flinched. What was she doing out at a time like this? Perhaps the dog couldn't sleep without that final walk of the day?

Joe landed on the tree lawn, rolled across the sidewalk, and came to rest on Pauline's front lawn. Nearby, voices cried out.

The little dog sniffed Joe's face.

"Is he all right?" The woman with the dog asked.

"I hope he's all right," Lina said. She was beautiful in her robe.

The cop took a knee beside Joe. "Son of a bitch, buddy. You out of your mind?"

Joe wanted to be close to Lina, and he reached out and touched the hem of her robe.

"Do you know this guy?" the cop asked.

"I don't remember his name but he was just on the roof outside my window."

"That's all I need to know," the cop said as he snapped a handcuff on Joe's wrist.

The policeman escorted Joe in the ambulance to the hospital. Joe felt fine. The cruiser had almost stopped in the road. It was Joe's own momentum that carried him over the hood and across the sidewalk. He might not even bruise. The cop didn't care.

"There are procedures," he said. "I play by the rules."

"That was my wife. At least she was supposed to be my wife. The wedding got messed up today."

"I heard about that," the cop said. "You've had a busy day."

"But I'm not stalking her, and I'm not a burglar. I want to see my girlfriend."

"Right now you'll see a doctor."

The hospital was St. Joseph, where he'd been earlier that day, and the Emergency Room bustled. People came in, people left, and people waited in the lobby. Everybody looked at Joe as the orderly wheeled him in on the gurney.

The nurse from before—the mean one, who threatened Joe—met them in the hallway. "I give you credit," she said. "I told you not to come back unless you're on a stretcher. You didn't disappoint."

FUGUE

The cop rattled Joe's handcuffs. "You've had a busy day."

Joe could only think of how Lina didn't remember his name, and hadn't seemed that concerned. A numbing dread washed over his face and down his chest.

The doctor confirmed that there were no serious injuries, and then the cop took Joe to the police station and locked him to the chair next to the cop's desk for processing.

"What am I charged with? Jay walking?"

"Reckless endangerment."

"Come on," Joe said. "Just let me go."

"I need to verify your identification. You didn't have your license."

"Can I make a call?"

"You'd better, if you want to get out of here soon."

The dread intensified and spread down his arms and legs. Reaching for the phone felt like moving his hand through mud. He wasn't sure whether to call his father, who was too drunk to drive, or his sister, who would laugh at him over the phone.

He realized he hated everyone at that moment.

The cop pushed the phone within Joe's reach. "Come on. What's the hold up? I don't have all night."

"I realized that nobody loves me."

"Tell it to the judge."

Lina awoke in her bed at her mother's house. She was confused but not disturbed. Throughout college, she and her friends had bounced around from one place to another before crashing, and waking up after such a night required a moment to get oriented.

This was different because another memory came to her. When she was a little girl, like four years old little girl, she would sometimes nap in the afternoon with the boy who lived around the corner.

She and this boy would walk with her mother to the burger place on the corner and they'd eat back at her house. Her mother would send them back over to the boy's house to play.

They'd settle down late in the afternoon while his mother sat in a chair to watch a movie on television. They would lie together on the couch and they would nap.

When she woke up from those naps, she'd have to look around to figure out where she was. The television would still be on, and the boy would be sleeping.

She'd lie there and wait until he woke up because there wasn't much else to do. That's what friends did.

She sat up in the bed—her bed in her mom's house in Shaker Heights, and not the couch at that boy's house.

She had this nagging feeling that the little kid she used to play with was the guy in the tuxedo who stood outside her house last night, who was hauled away by the cops.

So what happened to the guy in the tuxedo anyway? As Lina got up and looked out the window, she remembered the name Joe.

Outside, a Mercedes pulled into the driveway. Michael, her step-father, walked out of the garage and shook Harold's hand as he got out of the Mercedes.

This made her angry. It annoyed her she'd been having a nice memory about when she was a kid and seeing Harold and her step-father made her angry. But she didn't know why.

FUGUE

Joe awoke in the cell with his head resting on his arm.

The officer opening the door took a step back and waited.

His shoulder hurt from the odd angle and he felt sad. Why hadn't his father come sooner? "I have to go to the bathroom."

The officer pointed at the steel commode in the cell. "You can shit here, or you can shit somewhere else."

Joe sat up. "I'll shit somewhere else."

A different officer emptied the envelope with Joe's belongings and showed him the door.

Carl waited in the lobby and watched as Joe struggled with the suspenders.

Joe's sadness from before turned to annoyance. His father seemed bored. Shouldn't a father be angry, or concerned, or something, when bailing his son out of jail. "Aren't you going to say something?"

"You ought to return that tuxedo today."

"That's so helpful."

"I'm taking mine back so I could take yours."

"That'd be fucking great."

"What are you so surly about?" Carl asked. "I'm doing you a favor."

"That's it? Favors?"

"What then?"

"It seems like no one cares."

"I got you out," Carl said. "Do you want a ride home, or do you want to be a jerk?"

"Thanks for nothing."

"Fine then. Walk home."

"Fine. I will."

41

Joe followed Carl outside but stood on the sidewalk next to the police station as Carl continued on towards the parking lot. There was no way his father would leave him here.

Carl drove back that way and rolled down the window. "Last chance."

"Don't you even care how I feel?"

"I can tell you're being an angry asshole. Am I wrong?"

"I guess I am angry."

"Do you want me to kiss your ass? Would that help?"

"No. I want you to care."

"Grow up, kid. Do you want a ride or not?"

"No. Not if you're going to be like that."

"Fine." Carl rolled up the window and drove away.

The front room looked like a photo in a magazine with a high-backed sofa, stiff chair, a shelf with ceramic knick-knacks, and a baby Grand piano. But who even played?

Lina sat on the sofa with her legs under herself and the robe tucked around her body as Harold waved the pen light in her face.

"Any head pain?" he asked.

"The lump hurts a little when I touch it."

"So don't touch it."

"Thanks."

Harold sat in the stiff chair and crossed one leg over the other. "Your vitals are all good and the absence of head pain is, obviously, *un bon signe*."

"I still don't remember things."

"Is that stressful? I mentioned that I know an excellent therapist. *L'un des meilleurs*."

FUGUE

"Did I speak French and now I've forgotten it?"

"No. You didn't."

"Then why do you keep speaking French?"

"I find it more expressive."

Lina frowned. "You're the only one who understands what you're saying."

Harold smiled.

Lina shrugged. Maybe a smug smile gave him the confidence to be a good doctor.

"This is an interesting opportunity," Harold said as he moved across the room and sat at the piano. He played skillfully—and it was not unpleasant. "You can reinvent yourself. Figure out if you want to be the person you almost were."

Harold ran a scale but stopped on a sour note. He looked at Lina, then played a melody. It was familiar, the song, but Lina couldn't quite remember its name.

"Should I know that song?" she asked.

Harold shook his head. "I created it *pour vous et vous seul.*"

"Thanks, I think. First I need to figure out where I live."

Pauline walked in with a box of donuts, and offered them to Lina. "You live here dear."

"What? No. I mean my place. I remember having an apartment."

"That was college but now you'll live here for a while until you decide what to do with your life."

Lina waved away the donuts. "I didn't hit my head that hard."

"Don't tease," Pauline said. "You should stay with us until you get things sorted out."

Pauline looked to Harold and offered him a donut.

"No," he said. "The glycemic index in donuts is not favorable for me."

Pauline returned her attention to Lina. "Your father and I—"

"Step-father?" Lina said.

"Your step-father and I love you very much. This is your home. We can get you a larger bed."

"No."

"Lots of young people return home after finishing school while they sort out their first job, or first apartment. I was rather hoping, in fact, that you might rather do that so you don't make any other hasty mistakes."

Lina bit into a donut. "I remember graduating college. I did, right?"

"Yes," Harold said. "You also got an M.B.A."

"I don't yet have a job, right?"

"No. That is, yes, you don't have a job."

"Okay. So why don't I remember where I lived?"

"I believe you lived with Joe."

"Joe?"

Pauline shook her head. "In Joe's house. In *Parma*. He grew up in it and stayed, like a rat who refuses to leave the nest." She took a bite of a donut and then threw it back in the box while she licked her fingers.

Her mother did that—biting sweets but never finishing them. There were always half-eaten cookies scattered around the house. "Does that make sense, living over there while going to college over here?"

"No it didn't."

"Don't judge me."

"Then why bother talking about it?" Pauline took another bite of a different donut. "You were in a state of rebellion. I swear you only dated him to hurt me."

FUGUE

Lina pulled away from Pauline. "That is a terrible thing to say, even if I don't remember it. I would never do such a thing."

"Once you see his awful little house and the disgusting neighborhood, you'll understand what I mean."

"I was going to marry Joe," Lina said. "I must have been happy there."

"Easy for you to say," Pauline said. "You've wiped your memory clean of the whole affair."

CHAPTER SEVEN

Joe staggered into the condominium complex. There were nice, new cars everywhere. Back in Parma, his rusty Dodge Dart blended in with the crowd. The closest thing to sweet rides in his neighborhood were the retired auto workers who scored Cadillacs at some point and nursed them along until either they, or the car, dropped dead.

As he checked the numbers on the buildings a young lady stepped out of her condo and walked to her Acura coupe. She wore jeans, a breezy blouse and large sunglasses, her heels clicking on the cement.

She did not so much as even glance at Joe. He looked like a clown without makeup in his disheveled tuxedo—jacket clutched in his hand and dragging behind him, shirt untucked, suspenders dangling.

He watched as she drove out of the parking lot, chatting on her phone, her world in order like a red carpet unrolling before her feet.

He hated the East side people.

At last he found Rhonda's condo and knocked. She opened the door and stared at Joe. "Are you all right? You look like you haven't slept."

"The good news is I wasn't raped in prison."

"Well it was your wedding night," Rhonda said. "It would have been nice for you to have sex."

Joe tried to come in but Rhonda held fast to the door. "I don't think so," she said.

"What the hell are you talking about?"

"I don't want you in the house I paid for."

Joe pushed his way inside. "What's that supposed to mean?"

"You're living in Dad's house and you don't pay rent."

"So what? He doesn't care."

"I care."

Joe examined Rhonda's nose. Either the bandage was smaller or her nose was bigger. "Your nose looks terrible."

Rhonda flipped him off as she left the room. Joe admired the plush carpet, the clean walls, and the new furniture. It even smelled new, like fresh squeezed limes and rose petals.

"Did you redecorate or something?"

Rhonda, returning with a drink for herself, seemed confused. "No. I clean. And I take care of my stuff."

"For a year?"

Rhonda sat on the sofa. "Yes, idiot. That's what you do when you have your own things."

"I wish I lived in a place like this."

"Get a decent job and take care of your things."

"I was hoping Lina would do all that."

Rhonda nodded. "I know you're joking but also you're not joking."

"Relax."

Rhonda scoffed. "You sound so confident. What's the problem then?"

"Can I borrow your car?"

"No. What's wrong with yours?"

"It's crap. Lina's from a neighborhood like your God damn parking lot out there with bumper to bumper imports. My Dodge Dart screams West side."

Rhonda shook her head and pointed at the door. "Get out."

"What? Why?"

"I thought you needed help but to you I'm just a soft touch."

"Where is this coming from?"

"I thought this might make us closer as a family—as adults who can share problems and help each other. Instead, you make fun of my broken nose and ask to borrow my car."

"Why are you being like this?"

"What, a bitch?"

"No." Joe raised his hands. Anything he said might be used against him. "Please, help me."

Rhonda folded her arms. "Do you know why I'm mad?"

"Yes. Because I'm not giving you enough respect."

Joe sat on the sofa. His eyes closed and sleep beckoned to him, whispering in his ear.

Rhonda dragged a chair closer to the sofa. "You need to respect yourself more."

"I try to respect myself."

"You need to try harder. Dad lets you stay at the house so you'd have a place to stay. He expected you to get a job."

"I'm going to school."

"You've been going to community college for almost six years."

"Seven."

FUGUE

"There—right there—you seem proud to be the biggest kid at community college."

"I'm thriving at school."

"You're not challenging yourself."

Joe shook his head. "Do you have any idea how hard it is to take classes at a community college for seven years and not earn a degree. I spend half of my time figuring out how to make it all not work."

Rhonda waved her hand at him. "You're making a joke again, right?"

Joe shrugged.

"Okay, I'll let you borrow the car if you tell me about that thing that happened when we were kids?"

"What thing?"

"The thing with Lina's father."

"Why do you care about that?"

"I think it may help."

# # #

It started the summer after kindergarten. Joe and Lina had spent all of the days of kindergarten in the same way. Basically, every day of kindergarten is the same.

He thought the summer would be just more fun together, and he didn't even care if he saw any of the kids they met in kindergarten. He and Lina would have each other.

But Lina didn't answer the door when he walked across the street that first morning after school was out.

Joe was confused. They had all summer to themselves. But not if she wasn't home.

And if she wasn't home, where was she?

"She's at Wayne's house," her mother said. "She's been there all morning?"

"Wayne?"

"If you don't know who Wayne is, maybe you'd better go home."

His own mother didn't know of any new kids that had moved in. "Why don't you go look around the neighborhood," she said. "They're probably out playing right now."

Joe didn't want to go look. Joe just wanted to play with Lina, alone, until it was time to go get lunch.

Why didn't she understand that?

Wayne was a bigger, older boy who lived two houses away from Lina. Lina spent every day at Wayne's house. She didn't knock on Joe's door even once.

He waited all summer for Lina to visit. As he played by himself, he thought it would be better when school started and they'd be in first grade together.

But she was in a different class—with Wayne.

Joe wanted to play with Lina but Wayne never left her alone. Joe didn't like Wayne. Wayne could be mean.

Joe, watching from his front porch, waited for Lina to go outside alone but she was never without Wayne.

Joe ignored Lina like she ignored him, but it didn't change things.

Two years passed. Joe saw Lina at school but she had other friends. And she still had Wayne.

The summer that Joe and Lina turned eight, on a hot night with a storm coming in over the lake, there was a loud argument at Lina's house. Lina's mother and father shouted at each other.

FUGUE

"Stop it," Lina's mother screamed.

Lina cried.

The lights were on at their house. Lina and her mother staggered out of the house and held onto each other.

"Stay away," Lina's mother yelled.

Joe ran into the front room where his mother peeked out the window.

"Go back to bed," she said.

"I want to go see if Lina is all right."

"They're just arguing."

A gun shot! Joe heard them on television but he knew this was real.

Joe ran out the door.

"Joe," his mother shouted. "Wait. No—"

Joe didn't stop.

Joe ran across the road, past the Mazarelle's garage, and through Pindro's garden.

He stopped once he was in Lina's back yard. He hadn't been there in years and now he was again. It seemed so strange. But he had to know if Lina was okay. He had to help her.

There was light coming from the house. The plum tree was all in shadow and there was a bike leaning against the house and something else by the door. Joe crept closer.

"It'll be okay," Lina's mother said. She was around the other side of the house. They were somewhere on the driveway—

Joe tripped and fell on something hidden in the dark, but then the something moved.

"Pauline?" It was Lina's father. He was lying in the backyard in the dark.

"No," Joe said as he stood up. "I'm sorry."

"Pauline?" Lina's father waved a gun, raised his head but then fell back down in the grass.

Joe ran around the house and down the driveway.

He saw Lina and her mother on the sidewalk.

"It's okay," Lina's mother said. "It's okay."

Another woman, Mrs. Devala—Wayne's mother—ran to them and hugged Lina's mom, and then hugged Lina but Lina's mom kept them moving away from the house.

"He's drunk," Lina's mom said. "He's drunk out of his mind."

Joe was about to run after Lina when the police cruiser arrived. It stopped right there in front of the house and the cop got out and ran up the driveway.

Lina turned then to watch and she noticed Joe.

Joe waved to her.

Lina waved back.

Then Lina's mom grabbed her hand and pulled her along the sidewalk.

Before Joe could run after her, his own father grabbed him by the shoulder.

And that was the last time he'd see Lina for twelve years.

# # #

"You're screwed," Rhonda said.

Joe sat up and looked at her. She'd moved her chair next to the couch, out of his field of vision, like a shrink.

FUGUE

Joe thought she was taking notes on a pad of paper but instead she played a game on her phone.

"I pour my heart out and all you can tell me is that I'm screwed."

"We have no examples of adults with loving relationships in their life."

"Mom died. That's not Dad's fault."

"Even before she died, their marriage sucked."

It was true. Their Mom and Dad did nothing together. The closest thing to intimacy for them were meals. Once food was cooked, they each grabbed food and sat in front of the television. "You must have some advice. You like telling me what to do."

Rhonda nodded. "This is so messed up that by the time you figure out how to repair it, she'll meet someone else. You're better off moving on."

"That's terrible advice."

"How about dating a stripper? The redhead seemed to like showing you her boob."

"Nope. And I can't just give up on Lina."

"You gave up on trombone. You gave up on stamp collecting."

"I didn't love them."

"You love the Browns and you gave up on them."

"The Browns suck and don't deserve my love."

"Fair enough."

Joe laid back down on the sofa. "Why won't you help me?"

"I'll help," Rhonda said. "But tell me what Dad told you about the birds and the bees?"

Joe closed his eyes. It was important to recite the words like an incantation, exactly as Dad first said them, so that they remained Dad's words, and not his own. Joe cleared his throat. "You stick your pecker in a girl's vagina and that makes babies."

Rhonda cleared her throat, as well. "What he told me was, 'If a man asks you to suck on his pecker, tell him no.'".

Joe nodded. "What you're saying is that the advice from our father—"

"Fits on a matchbook."

"Great. So I'm screwed."

Rhonda squeezed his shoulder. "I have an idea. I don't know if it will help but you must promise to do what I say without question."

"Does it involve putting a pecker in my mouth?"

Rhonda raised a finger in warning. "You must promise to do what I say without question."

CHAPTER EIGHT

Lina discovered two long, shallow bins under the bed. The bins were packed with her summer wardrobe from the year before. She remembered moving things out of the old apartment, using this bedroom as a depot to hold things. The clothes were folded *just so* to fill the bin without crowding. Capris, slacks, shorts and shirts – like a walk down an Old Navy aisle.

She discarded the robe and slipped into a T-shirt and blouse combo and a pair of jeans. The comfortable reminded her of something.

That person—herself from fifteen months before—was not sure she wanted to finish her M.B.A., or if she wanted to work in finance at all, or if she should have kept up with equestrian because she showed lots of promise early. And she wasn't sure about Harold.

That person had been crazy about Harold at some point but once he was away, the craziness subsided. Was she crazy about the idea of Harold, rather than the actual Harold? Once actual Harold was unavailable, the idea didn't seem so great. Once actual Harold was away, at his residency, unable to talk on the phone, or visit, or anything, he didn't mean as much to her.

That was what that person pondered as she stacked Lycra blend jeans on the bed and pulled corduroys and fleece out of the bin from under the bed. By the time the T-shirts and shorts were stowed beneath the bed, and the sweaters and thick socks packed into her shoulder bag, that person decided to not worry about Harold so much. If he had wanted her nearby, he would have asked her to join him.

She might have gone if only he had—

"Can I come in?" Harold asked. He took a breath and looked her over. "Whoa. I didn't recognize you with clothes on."

That felt good, to have the doctor look her over like that. Maybe that's what she used to feel about him. "Time for another examination?"

"I tracked down the video of your, uh, the wedding."

"What wedding?"

"Your wedding. The one that wasn't the other day. If you're feeling up to it, you can see what happened."

"'We?' You mean you and the other doctors think it'll help my amnesia?"

"No. Your mother and I thought…"

Lina wrapped her arms around Marcie, the pink, plush unicorn. "I'm not sure I understand."

Harold took a half-step back out of the room. "It's fine. If you're not interested in seeing it, that's a strong indication you're not ready. Forget that I mentioned it."

Lina stroked Marcie's mane. "I am curious about a thing."

"Yes?"

"What happened with us."

"Us?"

"Us. We were dating, then we weren't, then we were, then you left for your residency thing."

"I was in medical school."

FUGUE

"But we were dating."

"The funny thing is, I don't remember a lot from that time. There is so much going on, and we hardly sleep, that it's all a blur."

"I think we were talking about getting married, weren't we?"

"We did at some point. Yes."

"But then…"

"Then you met Joe."

"Right. The guy I don't remember. And here you are."

"Who? Me?"

"I don't see you, or talk to you for a year and then you miraculously show up at my wedding."

"Small world."

"Were you stalking me?"

"I was invited."

"By who?"

"Your mother."

Pauline and Michael stood before the television in the den. Lina assumed they were conspiring. They did that, talk about things and then bring them to Lina together, with all the details worked out.

She glanced down at Marcie for support and the pink unicorn was there for her, as much as she ever was, without judging her or questioning motives. Marcie would never conspire against Lina.

Pauline pointed the remote at the television the way older people do, motioning with the remote, like speaking louder to a foreigner would help them understand your language.

But Lina didn't want to be negative. If she learned anything from Marcie's loving acceptance, it had to be to trust those who claim to love you.

"Look who's here," Harold said as he stepped into the den behind Lina.

"Ah, yes," Pauline said. "Good. I hope you're ready—"

"What is Harold doing here?"

"He's your doctor, dear."

"You invited Harold to my wedding without discussing it with me."

Pauline paused the video and crossed her arms. She smiled. "Yes, well, I knew he was an important part of your life."

"But I didn't invite him."

Harold touched Lina's arm. "I'm sorry. I had no ulterior—"

Lina pulled away, squeezing Marcie. "I'm just dealing with my mother right now."

Pauline sighed. "Please don't turn this into one of your things."

"My things?"

"Oh, there you go. I put a deposit down for both a church and a hall and you hated them both."

"Help me remember, mother. Did I ask you to do any of that?"

"No. You wouldn't even allow me to shop with you for the dress. And I was very disappointed—"

"Is that my wedding video?" Lina pointed at the television with Marcie.

"Yes, and you'll see how those fools—"

"Did you arrange for the videographer?"

"No. Yet another thing you forbid me to do."

Lina took the DVD out of the player and held it on her finger. "I bled for this and I'm guessing I paid for it."

Michael reached for the DVD. "We have every right—"

"I bled for this," Lina said. "Even if I don't remember it, I planned it, I paid for it, and I get to look at it first, by myself if I so choose."

Lina walked past Harold and out of the room.

"That is just typical," Pauline said.

Lina caught Pauline's look as she walked away. Better to say nothing more. Better still to get away and cool down. That was the only thing that helped with her mother problems.

She walked through the kitchen and grabbed the keys to the Buick as she went into the garage. She hadn't asked to borrow her mother's car but, given the circumstances, it was all she could do.

Lina backed the car out of the driveway, past Harold's Mercedes and into the street. She considered buckling Marcie into the seat but decided it would be fine not to do so this time.

As she buckled her own seat belt, she noticed her mother, step-father, and Harold run out of the garage after her.

But Lina didn't care to hear whatever it was they were yelling.

CHAPTER NINE

Lina knocked on the door. Maybe she should have called but she didn't have her phone. She had no idea, in fact, where her phone might be. Probably packed with other things for whatever would happen after the wedding she didn't remember.

She knocked again. It was the middle of the morning but what day was it? Sunday?

The door opened and there was Brittney staring at her. Brittney blinked and then her eyes went wide with surprise.

"Oh my God," Brittney said. "Did I forget to do something?"

"No—"

"Because I'm so sorry. I never can plan like you and then when the wedding went screwy there was, like, a dozen things I promised to do for you while you were gone."

"It's fine, Brit."

Brittney threw her arms around Lina and squeezed.

Lina felt like she didn't deserve a hug but what did she deserve?

"When you hit the floor I thought you were dead and then you were home before I could even get over there and *then* I heard you lost your memory."

FUGUE

"I didn't forget you."

"Awesome." Brittney pulled her inside and Lina felt her weight shift to Brittney, as if her own legs were beyond control.

"Are you okay?"

Lina looked at the shoes on her feet and couldn't remember putting them on. Was that normal? "I don't know."

They sat on the sofa and Lina hugged Marcie the unicorn. That was all she could think of doing. She had spent years being busy. Why not just do something useful?

"What's wrong with me? I shouldn't feel this way."

Brittney hugged her. "Tell me what you're feeling."

"I was fighting with my mom and then I ran away from her like some kind of loser. A better person would have done something about it. Now I'm just that person who hates her mom."

"Aw, sweetie, a lot of people hate your mom."

"Oh great. So they all think I'm just like her, and hate me too."

"Maybe not."

"I should have dealt with this years ago. I shouldn't have let her be the way she is. A better person would have fixed this."

"Yeah, well, you tell lots of people how to fix things, so maybe you can just fix yourself."

Lina pulled out of the hug and looked Brittney in the eye. "What do you think about me?"

"I don't know. I'm just saying that you offer a lot of advice."

"Great. I try to help people with problems but instead I'm an intimidating, intrusive interloper."

"At least you have a strong vocabulary."

Lina stopped herself from telling Brittney to fuck off. Brittney could only take so much. Maybe she *should* tell her to fuck off; that's the same thing as with her mother and that lack of commitment might be what caused her grief.

Brittney adjusted her seat and took a breath. "So you tell people what to do, a lot. It's not bad. You're kind of like a project manager, even when there isn't a project."

"That's a little harsh."

"I'm sorry but you're always about getting stuff done, right?"

"Yeah, because—" Lina stopped explaining. She needed to breathe.

"Are you mad now?"

"Seriously, Brit, you're just dumping on me." She sobbed. She didn't want to cry but the tears came on their own. "Are you trying to make me feel bad? I mean what the fuck?"

"That's not what I meant. Don't be mad. I don't know what I'm supposed to do here."

"Fine. Just quit telling me what a bad person I am."

Brittney took the DVD from Lina's hand. "What's this?"

"My stupid wedding. My mother sent Harold to go get it and they were going to show it to me. It pissed me off that they did it without asking first."

Brittney chuckled. "I know better than to do that."

"God damn it. You're dumping on me again."

"Okay. Sorry. Do you want to watch it?"

"I don't know," Lina said. "I'm not sure."

She nodded. "We could watch something else."

"Maybe."

FUGUE

Brittney pointed at a bottle on the end table. "Do you want wine? I find it helps me watch things on television."

Lina nodded.

The movie ended and the menu displayed on the television, recommending yet another movie. Lina's head hurt but it was because of the wine. Maybe she should eat something other than potato chips. "Do you have any Funyuns?"

"I think so," Brittney said and roused herself from the sofa.

They had been sharing a blanket, and the movement caused the empty bottle to fall on the carpet. An animal cracker box fell. When did they eat animal crackers?

Brittney returned with Funyuns. "What's up with Dr. Feelgood?"

"Harold?"

"Yeah. Are you going to lock that down?"

She lifted her head and stared until Brittney noticed that she was looking at her. "I was almost married just a few days ago."

"Yeah but you don't remember, so to you it never happened."

Lina looked back at the television. The Netflix menu was there but she could also watch the wedding. Her wedding again. But had she watched it already?

"Have I watched the wedding video yet?"

"I don't know," Brittney said. "Not here. Did you watch it with your mother?"

"No."

"Then no, you haven't watched it. Why do you ask?"

63

"Because for a second there I thought I had. It was like I could picture the scenes from my wedding."

"Wait. That means you remember. Do you remember?"

There were things she remembered, and they were definitely of herself getting married.

Brittney leaned in close. "Do you remember Joe?"

Lina nodded. The only truthful answer to that question was, "Yes."

Brittney hugged her. "Was it 50 First Dates? No. That movie is too funny to be instructive in any way."

Brittney picked up the remote and clicked through their recent movies. "Butterfly Effect was good but Ashton Kutcher was not, so, no, that couldn't have helped.

"Eternal Sunshine of the Spotless Mind was awesome but I was drunk and I forget what your reaction was.

"And it couldn't have been The Hangover or Mulholland Drive, because I couldn't follow either one of those."

"Brit—"

"So it had to be Memento. Did Memento restore your memory?"

It hadn't. Maybe it was like getting over a cold when you're a kid and you don't know what being sick is but you don't feel right and your mom tells you to lie on the sofa and watch television. She brings you soup and crackers and maybe some ginger ale. Two days later, you're better.

"I think I just remembered," Lina said.

"Oh."

"Don't be disappointed. Hey, you know how sometimes an idea emerges from your unconscious, like an answer to a trivia game you didn't even know you knew but then you say it and you know it's right and that you knew it all along."

Brittney frowned and shook her head. It was possible Brittney never knew such things.

"Never mind." Lina patted her hand. "I enjoy watching movies with you."

"Good." Brittney raised her wine glass in a toast and drank off what was left. "Do you want to watch your wedding and check your memory?"

"Yes. That's a great idea."

CHAPTER TEN

Joe lay on the sofa in the front room of his house staring at the television but it wasn't turned on. Who cares what's on. Nothing on television will get Lina back. The only comfort was the sofa itself.

This was the sofa where Joe and Lina napped when they were four years old, side by side, the scent of Play-Doh and grass in Lina's hair. Her neck still damp with sweat from their play, a smudge of dirt from when she rolled down the hill.

When they met again, twelve years after her abrupt departure from the neighborhood, he asked why she'd stopped playing with him. Was Wayne just that much more fun?

The answer was far simpler and made him feel far more foolish. Her mother insisted she play with Wayne. "My mom didn't like your mom," she had said. "And then you wouldn't talk to me at school."

When Joe admitted playing hard to get, she gave him a hug. It was a hug intended for that six-year old boy, but it helped a lot. And then she agreed to go out to dinner. Even if it was a pity date, Joe didn't care. He told her what she'd missed in the old neighborhood. She laughed at his jokes. He laughed at hers. Joe had messed around with a few girls but this was his first real date. He couldn't imagine having a better date.

To top it off, he reminded Lina about their naps on the sofa and she remembered. She admitted thinking about them, and how much fun it was.

The next afternoon was their second date, a bike ride and picnic in the park near the old neighborhood. Lina agreed to stop by Joe's house. But she suggested the nap on the sofa herself.

As they lay together on the sofa, Lina's hair held down by the sweat on her neck, Joe realized it might work. She might just like him as much as he liked her. He didn't have a job and wasn't close to finishing school, but that didn't seem to matter. She seemed as happy with him as he felt with her.

Now, as he lay there alone, he hoped she would remember their time together as kids. Then she might remember how good she felt with him. It had worked once, it might just work again.

But even if her remembering didn't lead her back to him, he hoped she would remember because it was a happy memory, and everybody needed a few of those.

A moving van, white with black lettering, pulled up to the curb outside. It's top was visible through the window, and Joe sat up to have a better look. The lettering on the side said, "We Move U." But who was moving?

Harold's black Mercedes pulled into the driveway. Harold, Pauline and Michael got out and looked at Joe's house.

Joe did not want visitors right now. He wouldn't answer the door. If he didn't answer the door, he wouldn't have to deal with them.

He peeked out the window and watched Pauline walk up to the door. But instead of knocking, she opened the door and came in.

Should have locked the door.

"Is she here?" Pauline asked.

"Who?"

"Who do you think?" Pauline walked down the hall, calling Lina's name.

"What's wrong?"

Harold leaned against the open door. "She left Pauline's house and we don't know where she is."

"How? When?"

Pauline walked into the kitchen, her footsteps like hammer strikes on the asbestos tiles. She walked back, glanced up the stairs to the attic. She frowned.

"Is the upstairs finished?"

"Sort of," Joe said. "My old man put down flooring and walls. It was only for storage but there's a bed."

"Joe." She turned to Harold. "My first husband's name was Joe." She sighed and motioned up the stairs. "My Joe always meant to finish the upstairs. He had plans for it, I suppose, but he never did a thing. It was exposed rafters and insulation, all those years, so we couldn't use it."

"Was the layout similar?" Harold asked.

"Identical. All these houses, everywhere in almost the entire city was built like this. You have to bulldoze them to the ground to make a change. It's like I'm in my home."

Joe glanced outside where Michael was talking with two men from the moving truck.

Pauline snapped her fingers and looked Joe in the eye. "Have you made any changes?"

"Not in the past twenty years."

FUGUE

"Of course not. That would take initiative, planning, and money. You have none of those."

"Hey," Joe said. "This is my house."

"Don't take offense. We both know it would be a lie."

Pauline went down the short hallway and looked in the two bedrooms. "Where did your sister sleep?"

"She shared the big bedroom with my mom. My father slept in the attic."

"A Polish divorce."

"They didn't divorce. My mom was sick, then she died."

"Please, spare me. My husband was Irish and drunk, as cliche as the day was long. And I knew what went on in all the houses. There were no secrets on this street."

This visit had gone on too long already. "What do you want?"

"Is this the only bathroom?"

"My father built a shower in the basement, next to the washing machine."

Pauline nodded as she returned to the front room. "He likely played cards down there with his chums, drinking, and they urinated in the shower or the stationary tub—if your mother was lucky."

"Why are you here?"

"Perhaps part of the attraction was the nostalgia." Pauline looked Joe over and shook her head. "We left so abruptly."

"Why aren't you looking for Lina?"

"Her things," Pauline said. "Is her cell phone here? Where are her school papers and personal effects?"

Harold said, "We're looking for points of contact she may have made, and then—"

"Do you mind if I retrieve my daughter's belongings? I want to secure them for her."

"Is that to help her or hurt me?"

"Well she doesn't remember you and she is upset by the entire affair. I want her to heal but that may take time."

"Our first priority is to track her down and ensure her safety," Harold said.

"But she ran away from you," Joe said.

Pauline shrugged. "As long as we are here, I'm gathering up her belongings—those things which belong to her. Would that be all right?"

"I guess."

"She was just a guest here, correct? Her name is not on the deed, and she wasn't even paying rent, am I right? Then we'll just secure the few things I know she has purchased, which I verified with her credit card bills that I actually paid. Do you consent?"

"Yeah," Joe said. Anything to get the old battle-axe out of his house.

Pauline smiled. She strode to the open door and waved her arm. "All clear."

She stepped back into the room and touched Joe's arm. "My attorney assures me this is legal, so I thank you for your cooperation."

Michael and the two movers came into the room and Pauline pointed at the hallway. "Start in the larger bedroom, and mind the inventory, Michael dear." Pauline snapped her fingers at Harold. "I saw papers and personal effects in the kitchen, so, if you please."

Joe observed them for a few minutes but it was confusing. How could everything change so quickly? Even

FUGUE

when his mother died, no one so much as touched any of her things for six months.

Joe walked outside and sat on the front lawn. He watched the movers take load after load out to the van. He hadn't realized how many things Lina brought into the house in just eight months of living together.

And for every thing she brought in, some other thing had gone out.

All of the old stuff—the chairs, the tables, the chest of drawers—that his mother and father had gathered in their years together in the house had been packed into the basement or garage as Lina bought new furniture.

At the time, every new thing felt like something they did together, to create their own home.

But without Lina, the place wouldn't even feel like home. It would be a source of pain.

So was he even going to want to live there?

Rhonda had gotten herself out of there as soon as she turned eighteen, working a job and taking college courses at night, just to be away from it all.

Joe had stayed there even when his father left, moving to an apartment above the Pearl Tavern.

So why stay? What was so special about a crappy little house in a tired, old neighborhood?

Maybe it took an hour and then Michael presented Joe with an inventory list on a clipboard and asked him to sign it, an acknowledgment of reclaimed property or some such bullshit.

Joe's hand, gripping the pen, hesitated over the paper. He may as well be signing his own death warrant, because there wasn't much left living for without Lina around. Even if she showed up now, would she want to stay?

Would she even realize that the crummy little house was her home? It wouldn't look like Joe lived there, now.

Pauline took Joe's hand in her own and helped him to sign the paper on the clipboard.

Pauline bent over to look Joe in the face. "If you hear from her, or if she stops by looking for her things, please tell her to call me."

Joe moved to the front steps but could go no further. What did it matter, anyway, whether he was inside or out? He thought maybe he should go help look for Lina but Lina probably didn't want to be found. And what would he say, anyway, if he found her? 'You don't know me but I'm the guy arrested on your front lawn. Marry me?'

Better to just wait.

His father came over and watered the lawn. It was a thing for Carl, to make his way across the lawn in summer with a hose in one hand and a bottle of Pabst in the other. Living in the room above the tavern, this was the one thing he missed about the house.

Carl pulled the hose from the back of the house to the front and sprinkled.

"Why do you do this?" Joe asked.

"It needs it."

"Not the lawn. Why do you hang around me but not say anything."

"What do you want me to say?"

"I want you to give a shit about things."

"I give a shit."

"Great."

FUGUE

Rhonda's black Lexus pulled into the driveway. And she walked around the water spray to sit next to Joe on the front steps.

"Did something happen? You weren't answering the phone."

"Lina is missing."

Rhonda leaned back in surprise. "Missing? As in Pauline doesn't know where she is?"

"The police are looking for her but there's no sign of foul play. She got in the car and drove off, so they have a bulletin out or whatever. But they're not dragging the harbor for her corpse or anything."

"That's a terrible thought." Rhonda smacked him on the arm. "Don't think like that."

"I don't know what to think."

"I'm sorry."

"Also, Pauline and Dr. Mercedes removed all of her stuff. They hired two guys to carry it into a truck and then they drove away."

"Were you not here?"

"I was here."

"Why didn't you tell them to get the hell out and leave the stuff alone."

"It's not my stuff."

"But what if Lina remembers and stops by? That won't look good."

"I didn't think of it then."

Carl made his way closer to them with the hose.

"I told him watering the lawn is therapeutic," Carl said. "When was the last time you watered the lawn?"

"Never, Dad. The last time was never."

"What are you going to do about it?" Rhonda asked.

"What do you want me to do about it?"

73

"I don't want you to waste any more time."

"I'm not doing anything until I know where she is. She may come back here."

"So do something positive."

"There is nothing I can do at this point."

"Get a job," Carl said.

Joe flipped off his father. Carl shook his head.

"He's right, you know," Rhonda said. "Maybe not today, and maybe not tomorrow but, at some point, you must get a job."

"But she loved me. I know she loved me."

"Yeah, okay. Being in love can be like heroin, or so I'm told, but it wears off. To have a lasting relationship, you must do something, like work. Maybe not get a job in business like she wants but find something you want to do. Something you can own. Something that says you want to be in partnership with her. If she wants someone to hang around all day on the couch and nap she'll get a cat."

Joe shook his head. "That's just great because there is nothing I want to do. I've ruined everything. Maybe doing nothing is my best move."

"Do you want to just go to the bar now with Dad and give up?"

"Can I do that?"

CHAPTER ELEVEN

Rhonda went in first and moved through the tables to the bar. Joe lingered by the door, giving his eyes a moment to adjust. There was glare from the windows and colored light from the neon signs along the wall. The middle part was dark, even with the lights on. In the far corner was a bowling game, and next to that was the dart board. It was the same, friendly neighborhood bar he'd known all of his life but he still wanted to punch someone. Even if it was his father.

Maybe especially if it was his father.

The hulking shadows of men at the bar came into focus and became the familiar regulars—Ken the plumber, Larry and Jerry from the Ford engine plant, and retired Nick. Pete was behind the bar. None of them would be a bargain to fight.

Joe had never been in a fight but he felt like this day might be a good time to start.

Rhonda reached over the bar for the darts, rousing Pete from his perch in front of the television. Pete waved.

Carl was at the bar, near the dart board wall where he sat. "What took you so long?"

"Nice to see you, too, Dad," Rhonda said.

Rhonda practiced her throws as Joe made his way to that side.

MICKEY HADICK

Pete drew a Pabst from the tap and slid it along the bar for Joe.

"You hear about the wedding?" Joe asked.

Pete nodded and shrugged.

"You gotta' get past that whole thing," Carl said. "Put it in the past. Get on with your life."

"Jesus, Dad, you could have helped out."

"Whatta' ya' mean?"

"Couldn't you have gotten them out of there?"

Carl set down his beer and leaned closer to Joe. "They said you invited them. Now what the fuck would you have said if I asked someone you invited to leave?"

"I don't remember inviting them."

"Well maybe you ought to start there." Carl took up his beer and drained the mug, then shoved it to Pete for a refill. "Take care of your shit, kid. But if you can't water the lawn, I don't know how you'll do anything else, anyway."

"What the fuck," Joe said. "No one is helping me around here."

"I think you're better off without her mother."

"Okay Dad. Thanks for that."

Carl pushed the beer mug to one side. "Time to be a man, kid."

This was familiar to Joe. When he borrowed the car the first time and put a dent in it, Carl told him to be a man about it. And when he couldn't figure out what to do with his life after high school, Carl told him to be a man about it. But before any of that, when his mother died, and all he wanted was for his dad to tell him it would be all right, Carl told him to be a man about it.

But now, here in the bar, it didn't seem like his father had a right to say such a thing. "If being a man means I end up like you," Joe said, "then I'll just stay a boy."

Carl slapped him. Joe heard it before he felt it, and then the sting burned all across his cheek.

"Don't you want to punch me?" Joe asked.

"I punch men. I slap boys."

Joe threw a punch. He screwed up his face to get all the anger he felt into the punch but he was on the ground, sitting on his ass, holding his stomach without knowing if his own punch landed anywhere. His gut hurt like crazy and he couldn't quite breath. But he noticed that there was a picture of Jesus on the wall behind the bowling game. You could only see it from right there, sitting on the floor next to the bar. Anywhere else, and the scoreboard for the bowling game would block it.

The thing was, the picture of Jesus was the same one on the wall at the church where they were married. Both pictures came from the same distributor, whoever made their living selling pictures of Jesus to whoever the hell wanted one.

It didn't seem like Jesus was watching out for him, though. Jesus was just there, minding his own business, like anybody else that goes to church and then goes to a bar.

To Joe, Jesus was no different than Ken the plumber nursing his beer, or retired Nick, drinking Canadian 7 with 7-Up; Jesus was just another guy at the bar having a drink, keeping an eye on whatever happened there at the old Pearl Tavern.

Outside the tavern, Joe noticed that there were weeds in each crack of the sidewalk, and soot and trash along the curb. The storefronts were completely different from what they were when Joe was a kid and none of them looked right. Like the signs didn't match the store, and he had to stare at each one to be sure it was what it said it was.

The dry cleaner was now an adult video store. The drug store now sold six-packs and forty-ounce beers. The florist was now a medical marijuana boutique—that was the closest of all of them to the original. Only the Pearl Tavern and the Pearl Bowling Alley across the street were still what they set out to be. What could he learn from this neighborhood?

"Why didn't you say something to Dad," Joe asked.

"What did you want me to say to him?" Rhonda asked.

"Like maybe don't punch your son."

"I don't think he was too proud of that."

"Bullshit," Joe said. "I think the bastard wants to kill me."

Rhonda grabbed Joe by the shirt and pulled him into the street. "He doesn't want to kill you. He doesn't know better."

They waited in the middle of the road for a bus to pass.

"Why am I following you? You're not doing anything to help me."

Rhonda ran across the road and waited. Joe had to wait for the next break in traffic.

"You don't have to follow me," Rhonda said. "You can go back there and drink, or you can go home.

Joe waited too long in the middle and another group of cars had to pass by. You would think as run down as

FUGUE

this part of town was that there wouldn't be any traffic but there was a ton of it. Then again, nobody was fighting to pull into the parking lot and spend money at the crappy little strip mall. It was a barber shop, a liquor store, a church, and an adult book store. The bowling alley was the anchor but nobody was bowling at this time of day.

Joe crossed at last, and they continued toward the bowling alley.

Joe stopped before going inside. "You know those kids that are abandoned in the woods and raised by wolves?"

"What about them?"

"They aren't the lucky ones. They have to go through the rest of their life trying to act like a wolf in a world of people. They're probably never, ever happy again. The lucky ones are the kids that are eaten by the wolves. It would suck to die that way but, once it's over, it's over."

Maybe it was the stress of the past week, but Joe had a vivid memory of bowling with his father and mother one time. The lanes were crappy and old even then. The cheap plastic benches and the projected score sheets that seemed cool fifteen years ago seemed ridiculously old now.

"Do you remember that time?" Joe asked. "We bowled with Mom and Dad?" The place full of smoke back then, like a massive tobacco fire was burning, which was what it was, because everybody smoked back then except the kids. Now it still smelled like that but you couldn't see the smoke.

"No," Rhonda said. "You're remembering wrong. I didn't go that time. I wanted to go but Dad didn't want me here. Said it was too rough and that I wouldn't enjoy it."

"Are you sure?"

"Yes, God damn it. He took you all kinds of places I never got to go."

"That's weird. I coulda' swore you were there."

"I cried because you guys were leaving me behind and Mom slapped me for crying."

Joe tried to conjure that memory but he couldn't. He didn't doubt it but he couldn't remember any part of it.

Rhonda shrugged. "So anyway, no, I never bowled here with Mom or Dad as a kid."

"You didn't miss much."

"Fuck you," she said. "I still would have liked to have that memory even though you don't remember it."

"Okay," Joe said. "Relax. Let's enjoy this game."

Rhonda's next ball only picked up the four and the seven pins, leaving a mess. She stood at the return, tapping her foot.

"Are you pissed about this? It was just one time."

"A little. I guess I'm just salty about the whole thing."

"The bowling?"

"My childhood."

The next ball came out of her hand early, nearly crushing her foot, and only made it half way down the lane before coming to a complete stop in the middle of the lane.

"I don't think I've ever seen that," Joe said.

Rhonda pressed the service button and the guy behind the counter, a middle-aged man with a pronounced paunch, and sporting a soiled bowling shirt, walked up the lane and retrieved her ball.

"Thanks," Rhonda said. "Hey, were you ever married?"

The lane guy nodded. "Forty years, I guess."

"Is it easy being married that long?"

FUGUE

The lane guy shook his head. "Most days are like a seven-ten split. You'd better get one of the pins, because you ain't gonna' get them both."

"And was it easy to get your wife to marry you?"

The lane guy scoffed. "Well, she was more interested in me than I was in her. Then she beat me on the lanes, and I took notice."

CHAPTER TWELVE

Brittney struggled for five minutes getting the video to play.

Lina wanted to step up and get it working for Brittney but it'd be best not to do that this time. How many people thought of her as the bitch with all the answers?

When they were roommates in college, there had been no major fights but more than once Brittney had grown distant after one of their spats in the room. Lina hadn't worried then, as Brit seemed not to care too much about anything, least of all being lectured by Lina about putting away the drying rack in a timely fashion.

They had gotten along fine once Brittney got a job and her own place. Lina noticed how Brit took some of her advice about setting things up but maybe that hadn't been welcome.

Maybe she'd been a little too bossy with her friend.

"I think I got it," Brittney said.

"I know you will. It's cool."

"You must have gotten quite a konk on the head, because you've usually taken over by now."

Lina didn't want to fight any more. She wanted a friend. "Thanks for letting me watch it here."

"You're not mad at me?"

FUGUE

Lina shook her head. She couldn't stay mad at Brittney. Brittney might be the only friend she had left.

Then the wedding video started.

# # #

They were in the crying room. The miniature table and toddler-sized chairs stacked with bags and cases. It was just Lina and Brittney.

Brittney helped with the final touches of makeup and hair.

Lina can see she had her game-face on. The Lina in the video is serious. She ain't messing around.

"Was I stressed out?"

"No more than usual," Brittney said.

"Do I seem too serious to you?"

"Maybe. I look fat in that dress, right?"

"No, I mean always. Do I always seem too serious to you?"

"Jesus," Brittney said. "Don't make me answer that now. You're in a good mood."

Michael escorts Lina down the aisle. Still she looks serious, rigid almost, in her stride.

The gown is lovely. It flows but on the close-up, you can tell it's nothing special.

"I bought that off the rack, didn't I?"

"Yes but it was gorgeous. That was a great bit of shopping."

"Thanks."

"More than I can say for the groom's side of the church. Where did you meet him again?"

83

"Parma."

"Figures."

She was right. They are dressed more for a picnic than a wedding. Or a trip to the zoo. Like a trip to the zoo to clean cages. At least there aren't a lot of them in attendance.

The bride's side dressed for the occasion. They are prettier, handsomer, and better dressed.

Michael presents her to the groom and then takes his place in the pew next to her mother.

Pauline's dress is flawless but she scowls at Michael and then at the camera.

"Your mother don't look happy."

"I'm not sure I would recognize my mother happy."

"Sometimes, when you scowl, you look like that."

"Oh Jesus. Don't say that."

"At least Joe looks happy."

"Dopey, more like."

They are on the altar, bride and groom, holding hands. Lina still sports her serious expression. The groom seems almost giddy.

The pastor begins the service but a noise in back interrupts him.

The bride looks to the groom, and the groom looks over at the best man. The best man shrugs.

The pastor begins again.

"What was that noise? What happened?"

"You don't remember? I mean, you straight up don't remember what happened? For real?"

"No, I don't remember. That's why I'm watching."

"Let me refill your glass."

The pastor explains about love, how it does not envy or boast, and it isn't proud. It does not dishonor and it is not self-seeking. But when he mentions that it is not easily angered, there is laughter coming from the back of the church, out of view on the video.

What is on the video is the bride's face, and she's angry.

The bride turns to look at the noise but the groom takes her hand and she returns her look to the pastor.

"I think Joe was drinking."

"What about the Best Man?"

"He was definitely drinking."

The pastor mentions that love does not delight in evil. His voice trails off as he looks up at the wedding guests. Then the pastor looks at the Best Man.

The bride looks over one shoulder at a guest and turns the other way to look at the disturbance. The video swing across the wedding guests and finds two women at the back.

The two women are dressed in tight dresses that show their boobs and tattoos. Their hair teased up and they check each other's makeup before realizing they are being watched.

"The two girls didn't seem drunk."

"But why were they there?"

"You'll have to ask them."

There are giggles coming from the back of the church and the video swings back around to capture one girl in back—the blonde— standing in the pew, her too-tight dress unzipped on the side. The camera zooms in to see most of her boob spilling out of the dress, like the good part of a muffin escaping from the baking tray. On her torso, revealed by her raised arm, was a dragon tattoo in bright red.

"Strippers? Are they strippers?"

Brittney pointed at the video screen. "I think that's what I say next."

Back on the altar, the bride, turned around, has seen enough. Then hell is unleashed.

The video pauses.

Lina, staring at the television, points the remote control at it but otherwise doesn't move. "I can't believe what I saw."

"I know," Brittney said. "I look so fat."

Lina was aware that Brittney took the remote from her. And also aware that Brittney refilled their wine glasses. Still, she could not think of anything to say. It made no sense.

"Do you want to stay here for a while?" Brittney asked.

Lina nodded.

"Do you *not* want to talk about what happened?"

Of course.

"Netflix binge?"

She nodded again.

"Awesome."

CHAPTER THIRTEEN

Rhonda treated Joe to an Indians game at the stadium downtown. Joe settled into his seat and focused on his Cracker Jack.

"You're welcome," Rhonda said. "Do you want a beer?"

"Not yet. But after."

They were in the upper deck, high above right field. The players on the field far enough away to be toy-like but you could follow the game. The Indians were playing the Tigers, so that was cool. Much of the big television screen behind center field was lost to them but still it was cool.

"Can I have ice cream?" Joe asked.

"Sure."

"Why are you being so nice?"

"When am I not nice?"

"It's not that you're not nice. But sometimes you get a little pissy about spending your money on me."

Rhonda looked at him and drank her coke and ate a peanut. "I'm just trying to have a good time with my brother, okay?"

"Sure. Whatever."

Rhonda ate another peanut, dropping the shell to the ground. "What whatever?"

Joe emptied the box of Cracker Jack into his mouth and chowed the crumbs down. "It's just that you get annoyed when I don't pay my fair share."

"You explained it yourself," Rhonda said. "You never pay your fair share. It's just that simple."

"But why does that anger you?"

"Because you don't pay your fair share."

"Yeah but you've always had more money."

"So that means you do fewer things, or get less stuff."

"Come on—"

"But in your case," Rhonda said, turning in her seat to face him, "it means you take Dad's old car and drive that. And you live in Dad's house, which he can't sell because you're there, and so he has to keep working."

"Dad likes to work."

"Dad is way past retirement age but he keeps working because of you. In a salt mine. The Romans used salt mines as prisons. That was the only job he could get."

"All right, I get it. But I think Dad likes working."

Rhonda turned away.

"So now you're mad?" Joe asked.

"Yes."

"Why did you even bring me?"

"I thought you might appreciate it. But you assume people with more money will take care of you."

Now it was no fun being at the game. The Indians were losing, they were too far away to see the field, and it was a pain in the neck to turn around to look at the Jumbo-Tron. The night was a waste.

Joe got up and stepped into the aisle.

"Where are you going?" Rhonda asked.

"To get a better seat."

FUGUE

They were in the last section of right field, and above them were the executive suites, attached to the face of the upper deck and circling the field. Inside one of those they gave you a hand job while pouring your beer, and sucked you off while they handed you a plate of food. You didn't have to watch the actual baseball game in the suites. You watched the televised game, instead, while drinking booze and having sex to music. Who cared about baseball if you could be in a suite.

Below them were the better seats of the lower deck. The ones close to the field were stupidly expensive, like a hundred dollars a seat, but that was the best place to watch a game. If you were that close, it was more like going to the city park and watching your friends play. You got a real sense of the game.

Way the fuck up in the last row of the last section in right field, all you could do was get into a fight with your sister. But those bastards by the fields, they could enjoy the game, and enjoy their beer, and enjoy their pretty girl-friends.

It wasn't fair.

Joe walked through the stadium to the section behind first base. He rummaged in the trash for empty beer cups, filled those with water, and then held them precariously in his hands—four big cups full to the rim—and he approached the usher guarding the aisle.

"Ticket, please," the usher said.

"Sorry. It's in my pocket. I got stuck buying drinks."

The usher smiled and nodded. "Okay."

Joe kept it casual as he made his way closer and closer to the field. It was the fifth inning, the game was all but out of reach already and most of the section was empty.

There was an entire row, right up against the field, empty, and Joe sat down in the middle of it.

Across the aisle was an older guy with white hair and a pot-belly. The guy wore a sweater and dress pants. Who the hell wears something like that to a baseball game? There were worse dressed guys at Joe's wedding than this guy at the game.

Next to the older guy was a young lady. Young enough to be the guy's daughter but dressed like she was his hooker. She was pretty and probably wasn't all that bad of a person. It was annoying as hell to have to sneak into a section to watch a crappy baseball game when this guy seemed rich enough to buy the team.

Joe noticed an official-looking hat on the seat next to the older guy. It was blue and had Chief Wahoo's face emblazoned on the front. It didn't look like a hat that guy would own.

So Joe walked over and picked up the hat. He returned to his seat and put the hat on his head.

"Excuse me," the guy said. "That's my hat."

"Oh, sorry," Joe said. "I thought it was mine."

The guy got up and walked across the aisle holding out his hand for the hat. "Give me the God damn hat."

Joe handed it to him. "Relax, buddy. Honest mistake."

"Honest my ass." The guy moved back toward his seat but then thought better of it and got into Joe's face. "You think you're some kind of a funny guy?"

"Take it easy, Grandpa. Don't short-circuit your pacemaker over a silly hat."

"Why'd you want it if you think it's silly."

"I told you I thought it was my hat. I got it as a souvenir of my wonderful evening at the stadium."

FUGUE

The guy's face twisted. "Fuck." He stood up and looked around but there was an usher already sliding into the row behind Joe.

"Is there a problem?" the usher asked.

"Yeah," Joe said. "This old fart has bad breath but doesn't have the decency to eat a mint."

And that's what started the fight.

CHAPTER FOURTEEN

Down in the flats, the dock for the cruise was at the end of the taverns and night clubs along the river. Farther inland was the remnants of the steel mills and factories.

Before him was a double-decker boat, like one of those sight-seeing buses but floating on the river.

Behind him there was one mill still in operation. Blue flame jetted out of a series of chimney stacks, burning off the fumes. The orange glow of the forge reflected off the smoke suspended above the valley.

The place smelled like flaming dog shit, and Joe was sick of it. He was sick of the lame clubs downtown, sick of the crappy sports teams, and sick of not having a decent, easy job in a nice office. The whole city, and his pain-in-the-ass sister, was driving him nuts.

Rhonda returned from the ticket office and sat next to Joe on the bench.

"Quite the view," she said.

"I've seen enough. Can't we go home?"

"I missed the end of the game because of you. And I got you released from the security office. I think you could do me this one favor."

"This is so unfair."

"Life isn't fair," Rhonda said. "But I think this is just."

FUGUE

"Just? Just what?"

"Justice. I think justice will be served if you do this with me."

"Fuck justice. This is a big pile of crap."

Joe stood up but Rhonda grabbed him by the shirt. "You picked a fight with a season ticket holder, wrestled a sixty-year old usher, and then ran across the field during the game trying to escape."

"So?"

Rhonda stood up, tightening her grip on his shirt. "I wanted to do something with you and you screwed it up. Now you'll do this with me."

"But why go on a boat ride at night? That's stupid."

"It offers a view of the city."

"I hate the city."

"Too bad, because here we go." Rhonda pulled Joe towards the gang plank.

It was slim-pickings for the crowd. The boat seemed like it had seen better days and with only a few people boarding, it couldn't be worth the fuel to take it out on the lake.

Rhonda led him to the upper deck and they sat along the rail in the warm breeze. She looked up at the skyline.

"Maybe this is just a fun thing to do," she said. "Maybe we won't ask any questions."

"Maybe I'll just sleep."

Joe understood that it was a pleasant evening but he didn't give a fuck. Rhonda gaped at the skyline and mentioned the twinkling stars. The moon hung above the lake and the reflected streak of light ran right into the mouth of the river. And behind them, the exhaust flames from the factories reflected on the river, as if the Cuyahoga was once again on fire. Rhonda, giddy as a goofball, said, "Isn't it lovely?"

"It's great," Joe said. "But none of this helps me with my problem."

Rhonda smiled. "From what I've seen of people who get married, they all hate each other anyway. You started with that."

Joe wanted to punch her.

"Come on, I'm kidding." Rhonda grabbed his arm but Joe pushed it away.

"Thanks for nothing."

"Most people don't even like themselves. And when you have to live with someone, once the honeymoon is over, you hate them."

"Jesus," Joe said. "Never mind." He walked across the deck to the opposite railing, and looked at the drunks on the docks outside the bars along the river. They all seemed happy. Maybe the secret of happiness was to never sober up and only spend time with other drunks.

The boat made its way out of the harbor, bore out onto the lake a few hundred feet, and then turned to run parallel to Lakeshore Park. Lights in the park shone on a softball field, a game in progress. What was softball but a way to kill time before going to the bar.

A small jet made its approach and landed at the airport as music drifted over the water. The music had to be from one of the clubs on the river. Joe thought he recognized the song, but couldn't quite recall its name

FUGUE

The half dozen tall buildings defining the Cleveland skyline rose prominently against the light of the city beyond.

Rhonda sat down next to Joe and hugged him.

"What is your deal?" Joe asked.

"Do you want to know the secret of staying together?"

"No. You're painting a shitty picture of life and I don't want to hear it. I need help winning her back."

"The secret is, stay close by."

"That's it?"

"That's it."

Joe covered his face with his hands. "How is 'stay close' supposed to help me?"

"Stay in touch with her, get a job like her job, or near her job, or eat at the same restaurants."

"That's all you got?"

"It's as simple as that."

Joe shook his head. "You said you would help me but instead we're traveling all around the city doing dumb stuff and your great nugget of wisdom is to 'stay close?'"

Rhonda shrugged. "I never got to do this stuff as a kid. I always wanted to hang out at the bar, go bowling, go to a game, and go for a boat ride."

"Son of a bitch. You've been taking me on a wild goose chase?"

"Okay, asshole," she said. "Now I'll tell you how to win back Lina."

"I can't fucking wait."

Rhonda leaned against the railing and pointed at the river, back in view as they came about for another pass at the city. "You know why the river caught fire?"

"Yeah. They dumped flammable shit in the river."

"Correct. They filled the Cuyahoga with trash, building materials, chemicals, and oil. They treated the river worse than a toilet. So it ended in disaster. That's your relationship with Lina, like a river that's on fire."

"What does that even mean?"

"Put out the fire and clean up the mess. Then you can have a river again."

"That's it? That's nothing."

Rhonda grabbed his shoulder. "Did you think you'd be able to attend community college forever?"

Joe pushed her hand away. "I'm doing fine in school."

Rhonda grabbed his shoulder again. "Did you think you'd be able to drive Dad's car forever?"

Joe pushed her hand away again. "The car sucks, so don't worry about it."

Rhonda put a hand on both of his shoulders and tried to make him look at her. "Did you think you'd be able to live in Dad's house forever?"

"The house ain't no bargain either." Joe bent forward trying to loosen Rhonda's grip but she pulled on his shoulders.

So he pushed.

She grabbed harder, so he shoved.

Then she kicked him in the face and she was gone.

For an instant he was furious—she kicked him!—then he realized that she'd tipped backwards over the railing. The kick in the face was her foot clipping him as she went ass over head into the lake.

Joe stood up and reached but she was long gone. He saw her fall spread-eagle into the lake, swallowed by the dark water.

FUGUE

He ran to the back of the boat and looked at the wake flowing out behind them but there was nothing but churned froth on dark ink.

CHAPTER FIFTEEN

Brittney scrolled through movie suggestions but then put the remote aside and took Lina's hand.

"I was thinking," Brittney said, "if you decide to not do anything about Dr. Looksgood..."

"Harold?"

"Dr. Harold. Do you think he'd go for me?"

That seemed like an odd question, even from Brittney. Lina took back her hand and twisted around to face Brittney. Perhaps it was the lack of light, or her own lack of food, but it seemed Brit had a red wine mustache and potato chip crumbs stuck to her chin. Maybe neither one of them was thinking clearly after the binge.

"I dated the guy for four years. It's not like we had one crummy date and I don't give a shit what happened to him."

"Okay, well—"

"And my marriage just blew up before it started. You stood there next to me as it exploded in my face, like my body shielded you from harm. You were a part of it, even if you didn't do very much to help."

"What? Do you mean with the planning, or with the disaster, because—"

"Either one. I'm thrilled you were there for me but you weren't really there for me."

FUGUE

"Sorry." Brittney pulled one of those potato chip crumbs from her chin and dropped it in her mouth. "I didn't know you were that upset with me."

"I guess I'm confused why you'd ask about Harold at a time like this."

"He looks hot."

"Yeah but you're my friend. You were my God damn Maid of Honor."

"Relax. I get it. You're always so uptight. It was just a question."

Lina threw aside the blanket. "That was not just any question, Brit. That was a huge fucking question."

"All right."

Brittney got up and went to her bedroom, slamming the door shut.

"Brit," Lina said. "I'm sorry."

But there was no response.

Lina lingered on the sofa. The Netflix menu now roamed across the television screen in screen-saver mode, bouncing from corner to corner. You couldn't see it on the video but she was certain that her head bounced off of the floor at church just like the logo on the television screen.

There was no reason not to watch the DVD of the wedding again. She was curious what else had gone on and Brittney hadn't asked Lina to leave.

Lina dropped the DVD into the player, retrieved that remote control from the folds of the blankets, and hit play.

As she settled herself back onto the sofa, she hit fast forward, blazing through the scenes of the crime.

Lina worked one scene in particular over and over. She played it, stopped, skipped back, and played it again.

Lina knelt before the television. Not like she might have knelt in church but like she was watching a bug on a stick do something interesting.

Except she was the bug, and the stick was the video of her wedding.

She stepped off the altar, stopped, ran, then fell.

With the sound off, it was easier to think of it like that —start, stop, run, fall.

Skip back and play it again.

Start, stop, run, and fall.

Skip back and play it again.

Start, stop, run, and fall.

She fell right there, in the aisle, next to her mother.

Skip back and play it again.

Run and fall.

Lina simplified it to what seemed the essence of the situation. She sprinted for just the briefest of sprints. Two, maybe three steps. Then she goes airborne.

Joe is right there behind her, filling the screen as she herself falls out of it.

Lina fell so quickly that the video didn't keep up. Lina moves out of there like a special effects swipe and Joe stands in the middle of the shot, his eyes wide with shock. Or maybe it's confusion.

But he couldn't have pushed her, even though he was reaching. It's clear he isn't that close. And he stopped as she fell.

FUGUE

Her mother, whose back is in the corner of the screen, seems close enough that, had she reacted quickly enough, she might have caught her.

Her mother, in fact, seems close enough to reach out and take Lina's hand.

Lina could not tell from that video why she had fallen. Her mother mentioned the high heels giving way but it'd be nice to see another angle.

Brittney came in at that moment. She burst into the front room like she was expecting something but didn't know what.

"What are you doing?" Brittney asked.

"Watching video."

"What video?"

"My wedding."

"Oh." Brittney's body tensed up even more. "You don't want me around."

"It's fine, Brit. I want you here."

"So I can watch my television."

Lina stopped the video. "What's the matter, Brit?"

"I don't stand up for myself enough. And that's my problem but I'm dealing with it."

Lina turned her body to give Brittney her attention. "Have you been in there thinking about this that whole time."

"Yes. Not everyone is as confident, poised, and confrontational as you are. I didn't get elected president of my class or anything."

"Brit, come on—"

"I think you should listen, for a change, instead of telling me things."

Lina crossed her arms but thought better of it and placed her hands in her lap. "Okay."

"If I decide I like Harold, and he decides he likes me, then you'll have to deal with it."

"All right Brit."

"That's it?"

"I don't want to lose you as a friend but, if we're both going to follow our heart, we may have to deal with it."

Brittney scowled. She crossed her arms. She seemed about to say something but, instead, she turned and went back into her room.

And slammed the door shut.

CHAPTER SIXTEEN

Joe drove Rhonda's car because she was in no shape to drive. Joe had forgotten that Rhonda couldn't swim, or he might have gone into the lake after her. But then maybe they both would have drowned.

"Can I stay at your place?" Joe asked. "I'm exhausted."

"I don't want you in my house," Rhonda said.

"So can I stay on your patio?"

"Sure."

"Can I have a blanket?"

"No."

"Come on. We got you out of the water."

"That fucking attitude of yours," Rhonda said. "That's what got you into this mess."

"Do we have to do this?"

"Yes," Rhonda said. "I told you I'd help you, and this is part of it. You did something stupid, and you won't even own up to it."

"Your falling into the lake was just as much your fault as mine."

"And that's why I don't think it'll work out for you and Lina."

"I'll tell you what," Joe said. "She'll remember me, and then we'll live happily ever after."

Rhonda laughed.

Joe tossed the car keys in Rhonda's lap. Screw her. There was no reason to laugh. It could happen that Lina remembers him, and that they live happily ever after. People do it all the time.

"Maybe you did Lina a favor," Rhonda said. "She only dated you to piss off her mother, like bringing home a black guy."

"Nuh-uh. She wanted to marry me and everything."

"She was on the rebound," Rhonda said. "If Dr. Wonderful hadn't broken her heart, you never, ever, would have met her."

"Bullshit. We grew up together. We are perfect for each other."

"Why would a beautiful, educated, career woman with the rest of her life in front of her want to marry a jobless college dropout?"

"You mean me?"

"Yes, you. Would it be because you have a bowling average of 218?"

"My average is 219."

"You weren't in the same social circles as Lina," she said. "You weren't in her economic class, and you weren't as educated. If pressed, I'm sure a linguist could identify enough pronunciation differences between Parma and Shaker Heights you'd be as different as a Canadian to her."

"We are from the same place."

"You grew up a world apart. Any reason is enough to stifle a relationship."

"She wanted to get married."

"You invited strippers to your wedding. Her wedding. The wedding to the woman you love—that's where you brought strippers."

"I didn't invite them."

"Well then you should have gotten them out of there."

"I tried."

"You should have tried harder."

Joe reclined the driver's seat. He would just sleep right there in the car, and there was no way Rhonda could make him leave.

Joe parked his car along the curb of his red brick road at the intersection near the hamburger joint. The car dieseled as Joe sat and stared at the restaurant. It was a small white shack with a red, pointed roof, and it was as much the thing that brought him and Lina together as anything. Without that restaurant, they may have had a different summer, and what happened with Wayne the next year may not have mattered because Joe wouldn't have fallen in love with Lina already.

The car quit dieseling and Joe got out of the car. He walked across the parking lot. From this angle, the restaurant showed its years. Paneling rotted along the side and back. Ventilation unit rusted. Cement walkway cracked and over grown with weeds. The newest looking thing was the garbage dumpster behind the back door.

An older man smoking a cigarette stepped out the back door and tossed a garbage bag into the dumpster. The old guy paused for a minute to take a drag, flipped the butt across the parking lot, and went back inside. It was possible that was the same guy who owned the place twenty years before.

Joe ordered a burger, fries and a shake. The old guy took his order and then, without washing his hands, turned around and cooked.

"How long have you worked here?" Joe asked.

The old guy set the sack of food on the counter. "Forever."

"Do you remember me?"

The old guy glanced at him but shifted his gaze to the traffic on the boulevard outside. "Do you owe me money?"

"No."

"Then I don't remember you."

Joe stepped out and glanced back inside. Would it kill the guy to ask why he thought the guy might remember him? Would it kill the guy to ask about his day? Would it kill the guy to smile?

At least he hadn't sunk as low as the old guy in the restaurant. Joe would still talk to people. And even smile, although he wasn't too keen on it at the moment.

The food might get him close, though, and his mouth watered as he got in his car. But the car refused to start.

Joe cranked the engine again, and again, and again but it wouldn't catch. On cold mornings it had this habit, but this was one of the nicest days of the year. When the battery at last ran out of juice, Joe abandoned ship.

Joe studied Lina's former house as he walked home. The new owners had done little. A new roof, a coat of paint, a few shrubs in the front.

Up and down the street, the houses remained the same in spite of almost all the original owners being dead and the survivors moving away. The neighborhood's most endearing and enduring quality was the unspoken rule of communicating with each other via silent stares and contemptuous looks at weed-filled lawns.

Joe flopped onto his sofa intending to savor the French fries and milkshake but stared at the ceiling instead.

FUGUE

It wasn't so different—staring at the ceiling—than watching TV. Shadows moved in the room with the sun, cars passed by on the street, and Joe was no more educated or entertained after an hour than if he'd been watching television. Or maybe it was two hours.

The front door opened and Lina walked in. "Hey," she said. "I hope you don't mind."

Joe sat up. "No. Not at all."

Lina looked around. There wasn't much to see. "Were you burglarized?"

Joe stood up. "Sort of."

"I came to get my stuff but maybe I'm remembering wrong. Maybe I didn't live here."

"You lived here but your mother beat you to your stuff."

"She took everything?"

"She didn't want me to have any reason to see you."

Lina nodded. "That sounds like Mom."

Joe stepped closer. "I care about you, okay?"

Lina backed towards the door. "Okay, I, uh..."

"Do you want a drink? Or to go get something to drink?"

"No but thanks."

"Are you still mad? Because I can explain."

Lina shook her head. "I don't think you can. I watched the wedding video and it's just ridiculous."

"I didn't mean for it—"

"You had ample opportunity to prevent what happened."

"I know but— wait, do you remember me?"

Lina nodded. "I don't remember what I was thinking, like why I thought it would work."

Joe's heart raced. The lump in his throat could either be a scream of pain or yesterday's lunch. He took a deep breath and raised his hands. "We laughed a lot together. Remember that?"

"I remember laughing."

"That was fun, right? Give me another chance."

"Joe, I think it's best if we don't see each other again."

"Remember shopping on Saturday mornings at the West Side Market?"

Lina shrugged. "It was nice, all of it, but—"

Joe forced himself to swallow and cleared his throat, trying very hard to not burst into tears. "Let's drive down to the lake and walk on the shore—"

"Okay. I know you're sorry, Joe, and I'm sorry, too but I only came for my stuff. I think it's for the best if we don't —"

"Rain check? Please just let me call you in a couple of weeks."

Lina shook her head and reached for the door.

Joe grabbed the bag of French fries from the floor. "Do you want fries? Remember how we used to eat these?"

She smiled. It was a look of pity and it took his breath away. The lump in his throat was now in the pit of his stomach.

"Goodbye, Joe."

She went out the door and closed it before he could take another step.

FUGUE

Joe ran down the street toward his car but stopped within a few houses out of breath and walked. Maybe half of the lawns were decent with nice, green grass. But the rest were crap, just like his. The city may as well rename the street to crab grass lane. Could you tell who was happy inside by how nice was the lawn?

He willed himself to run again but tripped on uneven sidewalk and fell. He stayed down for a moment—the pain was sharpest in his palms where he'd scraped them on the cement. The best looking grass in front of most houses was whatever sprouted in the cracks of the sidewalk.

Joe got up and limped to his car.

Inside, he prayed it might start but the ignition wouldn't catch. It wouldn't even sputter—the car would not start. He turned and held the ignition, spinning the starter until the battery died.

Now what?

He knew no one in the neighborhood to ask for help. He may as well steal a car.

Joe went into the restaurant. The old guy behind the counter looked at him but said nothing.

"Can I borrow your car?"

The old guy shook his head.

"It's an emergency."

"I don't have a car."

"Can I use your phone?"

The old guy shook his head. "The phone is only for customers."

"I was in here two hours ago and bought food."

"The phone is only for current customers to talk about food."

"It's an emergency."

"You mentioned. Do you want me to call the police?"

"How about if I buy a hamburger?"

The old guy lifted the phone and set it on the counter. "Who are you going to call?"

"My father. I'll ask if he's hungry."

The old guy pushed the phone towards Joe. "One minute."

Joe dialed the Pearl Tavern. Pete the bartender answered and put Carl on the line.

"Can you help me?" Joe asked. "My car won't start, and I have to see Lina."

"You want help?" Carl said. "Let me get you a job in the salt mine."

"No. I need to go see Lina."

"She has no respect for you until you get a job."

The old guy behind the counter tapped his finger on the phone receiver.

"Oh," Joe said. "Do you want a hamburger?"

"What?"

"Are you hungry? I'll bring you a hamburger."

"Sure," Carl said. "I could eat."

Joe was sweating like a pig when he got to the Pearl Tavern. The darkness felt good and he chugged the beer that Pete offered.

"What happened to you?" his father asked.

"I ran here," Joe said. "Well, walked."

"It's only two blocks."

"I don't run much."

"That's why you need to work with me. You'll get into shape."

FUGUE

Joe handed him the satchel with the burger. "You don't look like you're in shape."

"I'm strong as an ox."

"If I promise to come work with you tomorrow, will you let me borrow your car today?"

Carl bit into the hamburger and said, "No. I'm leaving in a minute to go to work. This is my shift. So let's go."

Carl jammed the rest of the burger into his mouth and lifted his car keys out of his back pocket.

Joe snatched the keys and ran for the back door. He didn't think he could run a hundred steps but the car was probably only fifty, and he only had to out run his father.

Joe stumbled in the bright light but didn't fall. He shielded his eyes and searched the back lot for Carl's Ford.

"God damn you," Carl said as he burst out the back door.

Joe saw the car and was in it and driving away before his father could stop him.

Then he was out on Pearl and on his way but realized he needed to make one stop if he had any hope of winning back Lina.

CHAPTER SEVENTEEN

The bachelor party was the most fun Joe had had in a while although some of the details were still a little fuzzy.

It was at the V.F.W. Post 2133 hall, same place as the reception. Gary knew a guy who had an uncle that could get them a deal. And for the bachelor party, the deal was that the guy and the uncle got to attend the party.

There was a lot of drinking. Gary knew another guy that could get them a deal on beer and booze and that guy stocked the bar in the corner with plenty of cheap stuff.

Carl planted himself at the bar. Pete the bartender from the Pearl Tavern was next to him, and the guy from the bowling alley was there, elbow to elbow with Carl.

Lina's step-father, Michael, was there but he wasn't mingling. He seemed more like a spy than anything else, keeping an eye on stuff. But he drank his share. He kept drinking 'seven and seven', Canadian Seven with 7-Up, more of a drink for kids rather than an orthodontist from Shaker Heights, but maybe that was his way of trying to fit in.

Joe's friends from high school showed up and also some guys he met during the six years he'd been going to community college.

FUGUE

It turned out that Gary knew yet another guy who had an uncle that ran a floating casino. That uncle pulled up in a truck filled with gaming tables and a crew to work the action. They had black jack, poker, roulette and craps.

The casino tables were crowded. They guys yelled, cheered, and laughed. It was a great bachelor party.

Then, two hours after the games started, the uncle cashes everyone out, they pack up, and they're gone. They never wait to see if the cops will show up.

Yet another guy Gary knew brought strippers. That's how Holly and Veronica got involved.

They were escorted by a thick-necked guy in a leather jacket. He plugged in a portable stereo and the girls danced.

A circle formed around the girls as they stripped. The thick-neck guy is never more than half a dozen steps from the dancing, so everybody keeps a respectful distance. Soon, Holly and Veronica are wearing nothing but platform shoes and their tattoos.

Then the thick-necked guy asks for two chairs, and the girls lap-dance for Joe and Gary. It was fun. They knew what they were doing. Joe was aroused. Veronica—the blonde one—straddled him.

She smelled nice.

"It's just vanilla lotion," she said. "Nothing fancy. Guys love it."

She took his drink from him, dipped his finger in it, and then sucked his finger. Joe liked it but he also didn't like it because that seemed a little more personal than just a lap dance. Even with her tits just inches from his face, sucking his finger seemed like this was pushing the limit.

But it felt nice.

Michael and Carl were next. Carl had to be dragged away from the bar but Michael was on the chair and smiling like a little kid at a birthday party.

Carl smiled as Holly danced on his lap but wouldn't let her take away the beer.

Michael, however, buried his face in Veronica's boobs, grabbed her ass, and grabbed at her tits. Veronica slapped his face before the dance was over, which drove the guys in the crowd a little nuts.

The thick-necked guy stepped in and ended the dance.

Then it was Joe's turn again but this time both Veronica and Holly danced for him, each one straddling a leg, writhing and squirming to the music. It was more lap and less dance, and they rubbed him and pulled his shirt off.

The guys chanted something at that point but Joe couldn't quite remember what it was. Veronica leaned into him and whispered something in his ear while Holly sucked his fingers one at a time.

Joe said something to Veronica and she laughed but he couldn't remember now what he said that made her laugh.

There was no way he invited her to the wedding because that wouldn't have made her laugh.

He wished he remembered what he had said to Veronica while she straddled his leg and pressed her boobs against him as Holly sucked each of his fingers. If he remembered what he said, he might convince Lina it all was a big mistake.

Gary had a place on West 110th, near the V.F.W. Post. Joe waltzed in and didn't bother to say hello.

FUGUE

"I need you to help me," Joe said. "I gotta' convince Lina it wasn't me that brought the strippers to the wedding. You gotta' tell her."

"I gotta' tell her what?" Gary asked.

"Tell her it wasn't me."

Gary sprawled on his sofa watching television. "Fine," he said as he sat up. "I'll tell her whatever you want."

"But you have to believe it."

"No, you want me tell her something. I'll tell her anything. I don't care."

Joe walked over by the sofa. This was classic Gary, doing whatever he felt like, not getting what the situation was about. The house could be on fire and he wouldn't know why you'd want to leave. "Believe it or she won't be convinced. If you just say something she'll know it's bullshit."

"But it is bullshit."

Joe threw up his hands. "How can you fucking say it's bullshit?"

"Because it is."

"But I didn't do that. I didn't tell the strippers to come to the wedding."

"I don't know that. I was drunk out of my mind. I probably told them, yes, but I don't remember shit."

Joe paced across the room. "You are so fucking useless."

"What do you want me to do?"

"I want you to help me."

Gary changed the channel on the television. "Listen to you. You're the one full of shit. Besides, you're better off without her."

"Fuck you Gary."

"Fuck you too."

"And you left me with the police," Joe said. "You're a piece of shit."

"Hey, anybody in my shoes when you get nabbed does the same thing. We take care of ourselves. So fuck you again."

"You didn't even bail me out."

"You didn't call."

"Fuck you."

Joe left. There was nothing more he could think of saying, and what he wanted was to punch the fucker. He'd wasted all of this time looking for help and got nothing but grief.

"Hey," Gary said. He stood on the porch, pointing the remote control at Joe. "You need to get fucked, you know?"

"Thanks."

"I'm serious. You need to go fuck something that will spread its legs for you. Quit worrying about yesterday's problems, man. Let's go have fun."

"Shut up."

"I'll call the strippers. I bet they feel sorry for you."

"Fuck you."

"Fuck you too," Gary said.

Lina parked the Buick in the garage. The other parking bay was filled with her things removed from Joe's house. Why the hell wouldn't they take it inside? Was her mother afraid of messing up her house?

Lina left the keys on the kitchen island. She should have washed the car but *too bad*. She could have also set it on fire and rolled it into the river.

FUGUE

And if her mother didn't have a good explanation for what she saw in the wedding video, she still might drop the car in the river.

"Mother?" she called.

"Lina?" her mother called from the den.

There Lina found her mother sitting on the sofa staring at more of Lina's things piled in the middle of the floor. "What are you doing?"

"Just sitting."

"Why?"

"I don't know. I've been worried about you and—" she blew her nose and then crossed her arms. "I've been worried about a lot of things."

Lina sat in the chair on the opposite side of the room. "So this is my stuff? Dumped on the floor, dumped in the garage. Is there another pile in the back yard?"

"Oh please don't yell at me. This has all been very difficult."

"I bet."

"And why are you so angry? You didn't even hug me."

"You didn't hug me."

"Oh for heaven's sake." Pauline got up from the sofa and stepped around the pile but waited for Lina to stand up.

Lina hugged her but just for a second. "What were you going to do with my things?"

"I don't know. I wanted them away from Joe Schmoe."

"That was my problem to solve."

Her mother sat back down on the sofa and pulled an afghan blanket around her legs. "I know you don't like to give me credit for things."

"I watched the video," Lina said. "The wedding video —"

"Of course the wedding video. I watched it too."

"But I took it."

"I got another copy," Pauline said. "What did you think?"

"Well fuck." Lina sat on the chair and crossed her arms. In front of her in the pile on the floor was her journal. It was leather-bound with an elastic band around the cover to keep it shut. She snatched it up and flipped through the pages to the most recent entries. She'd used it as a diary from time to time but only when she had been distraught. There was nothing in those last few entries about Joe or the wedding. In fact, flipping through the pages revealed nothing about Joe.

Lina held up the journal. "Did you read my diary, too?"

"You took off," her mother said. "I was worried sick. You didn't even take your phone. Harold is talking to the police about organizing a search. We were all worried sick."

"But did you read it?"

"One of us may have flipped through it searching for clues. We didn't know where you were."

"You didn't think to call Brittney?"

"I didn't have her number. I can't remember her last name to look her up." Pauline laid down on the sofa and pulled the afghan over her shoulders. "You didn't let me help you with the wedding plans. I was in the dark about the whole affair."

"Don't make this about that."

"What am I supposed to make it about? It's like you hated me and didn't want me there."

Lina used her foot to lift a stack of papers in the pile and saw her binder used for the wedding plans, along with several notebooks.

FUGUE

"I wanted you there, mother. That's why I invited you. But I wanted it to be my life."

"Fine. So what are you going to do next?"

"I'll sort out this mess."

Pauline blew her nose into another tissue. "I have bins and we can buy shelves."

"Not this mess," Lina said. "My fiance. My boyfriend. My wedding."

Pauline looked at her. "Your wedding? That seems cut and dry."

Lina studied her mother for a moment. She noticed a familiar disdain for eye contact. "When you watched the wedding video, did you notice anything about when I tripped?"

"What? I was horrified. We were all horrified. We wish it never happened but—"

"I noticed something. It looks like you tripped me."

"That's absurd."

"That's what it looks like."

Pauline threw off the blanket and stood up. "I refuse to be accused of such a thing in my home."

Lina jumped up and into the doorway blocking Pauline's dramatic exit. "It's a simple enough question."

"You're being ridiculous."

"Do you want to watch it right now? I can show you —"

"You have always treated me like this, like I'm an idiot. I don't know if it was because of what your father did to us, or something else I did but you are very unfair."

"So you don't even want to discuss it?"

"Who would want to discuss such a ridiculous thing. Now please let me get past you."

"Fine," Lina said, and stepped out of the way. "But now I know what I'll do next."

CHAPTER EIGHTEEN

Joe ran to the front door and went inside. He took one step down the hall and there was Michael, standing at the other end of the hall.

"What do you want?" Michael asked.

"Oh, I, uh—"

Michael charged and grabbed Joe by the shirt and walked him back out the door.

"Mr. Sabbath, I need to see Lina."

Michael let go of the shirt when they were in the middle of the yard and threw a punch at Joe's head.

Joe ducked it and ran back into the house, locking the door. As Joe walked down the hall, he heard Michael pounding on the door behind him.

"Now what?" Lina asked. She was coming out of the den, and Pauline followed her.

"Just what we need," Pauline said.

Joe felt his face smile and his heart flutter. Lina was angry but it was the most beautiful anger Joe had ever seen.

"Lina," Pauline said. "Did your little lap dog here give you this idea? I know he never liked me. No one liked us back in that pathetic excuse for a neighborhood."

"Please let me explain."

Lina shook her head, waved her hand to move him aside, and went up the stairs.

"Come back and talk to me," Pauline said.

"Will she come back?"

"If you'll shut up I may find out."

"Mother," Lina said from the top of the stairs. "Go out front and check on your husband."

"Why?"

"Because he's in a fist fight with Joe's father."

Joe ran up the stairs to Lina's room.

"We need to talk," he said. "Please?"

Lina looked at him, showing no sign of recognition. She zipped up a suitcase and shoved it at him. "Can you take this downstairs for me?"

"I need a few minutes."

Lina stuffed notebooks and folders into a backpack. "Take this, too," she said as she zipped it up.

"What are you doing?"

"I need to get out of here." Lina stuffed clothes into a duffel bag, then went across the hall to the bathroom and brought back her toiletries, which also went into the duffel.

Lina slung the duffel bag strap over her shoulder, grabbed Marcie the unicorn from the bed, and motioned for Joe to get moving.

"Where to?"

"The garage."

Lina packed the bags into the Buick, then rifled through her boxes taken from Joe's house.

"Lina, we need to talk."

"So talk. I'm listening."

FUGUE

"Well now I don't know what to say."

Lina looked over her shoulder. "That's it?"

"I want you to give me another chance but I don't know how to convince you to do that."

Lina handed a box to Joe and motioned for him to load it into the car. "You'll let me know if you think of that one?"

"Don't you have any sympathy?"

Lina paused at this. "I guess not."

She handed him another box and loaded one herself into the back seat.

Then she got in the driver's seat and started the car as the garage door rose.

Lina backed the car out of the garage and stopped when she noticed the sunlight in the trees. It was later in the afternoon, the sun was behind the trees and the maple next door and the oak across the street were moving in the breeze. The sunlight shimmered through the leaves as they danced where they were, reaching out for the light. It was like that on this street in summer, as the heat of the day wore on, the wind always picked up as the sun dropped.

When they first moved here, before she met any of the other girls in the neighborhood, she'd sit on the lawn, about in the middle and read a book, and she remembered noticing how the breeze picked up later in the day.

At some point she realized it was like a convection current, hot air rising from near the ground and cooler air sweeping in. But the Cuyahoga Valley had something to do with it, and so did Lake Erie, and then whatever else was rolling in from the West.

You could spend your life studying, trying to predict the weather, and you'd be wrong more than you were right.

There were far more things going on at any moment than she could figure out but she knew it was warm, and that a breeze was blowing, and the sun was setting. Knowing those things, she was fine with reading her book on the front lawn happy enough to not be in school. Why the breeze blew just as it did was too much to worry about for a little girl, or anyone, in fact.

Lina's gaze dropped from the shimmering light in the trees to the front lawn where her step-father sat in the middle of the lawn, about at the place where she used to sit and read. Her mother knelt beside him. They both looked up and stared at Lina.

At the curb was Rhonda and Carl standing next to a car in the street. She remembered their names straight off —Rhonda and Carl. She must be getting better.

They all stood and watched her. It was a moment of *deja vu*—but this never could have happened, everybody standing and watching her walk across the driveway.

Before her, in the garage, stood Joe. He seemed about to cry and she recalled a time in Kindergarten when a storm rolled in during nap time, and while most kids stood at the window to watch, Joe sat on his blanket, staring at the dark clouds, about to cry.

Even as a little kid, he was more of a project than a friend. Twenty years later and he still hadn't grown up. What did she ever see in him to let it get this far?

And so she took her foot off of the brake and continued to back the car down the driveway.

FUGUE

A horn honked behind her as another Buick pulled into the driveway blocking her path. Lina honked and waved for him to move but instead Gary got out of his car and walked around to open the passenger door.

"I'm here to help," Gary said. "So you're welcome."

Gary offered his hand to the woman in the car and helped her get out.

It was the stripper from the wedding. She wore skin-tight leggings, a tube top, and an open blouse tied off like Daisy-Duke. Her face and hair were done up as if she were about to go out on stage. "How's everybody doing?" she asked.

Lina could not believe what she saw. "You haven't disgraced me completely yet?" she shouted out the window. "Some shred of my pride you haven't soiled? Is that why she's here?"

Joe shrugged. He grabbed Gary by the shirt sleeve. "Why is she here?"

"I'll let her do the talking," Gary said.

The stripper strolled over to the car window. "You're the bride, right? I wanted to explain about the other day."

"I don't want to hear it," Lina said.

"But what if I wasn't the one to invite her," Joe said. "That's what I wanted to tell you, is that I don't think it was me. And I asked Gary to help explain that to you, because I didn't think you'd listen."

Lina sat still in the driver's seat. She had to be tapping her fingers against her thumb, which was never a good sign.

Joe looked pleadingly at the stripper. "That's why you're here, right?"

Lina got out of the car and approached the stripper. "Let's hear it. Tell me that Joe did not invite you to our wedding."

"Oh he invited me," the stripper said. "In fact he gave me an invitation." The stripper fished a folded and bent copy of Lina's wedding invitation out of the waist band of her leggings.

Lina tapped her fingers with her thumb, *index-middle-ring-pinkie*. She reached out and took the invitation. There was her name in a black, script font on a creased and smudged tan-colored card:

> *Mr. and Mrs. Michael Sabbath invite you to the wedding of Lina Kerrie Finnerty and Josep Donat Kryznk...*

Betrayed. Joe betrayed her. "Thank you."

The stripper produced a tube of lip gloss from her waist band and applied it to her lips. "I don't think you should be mad at him or nothing. You know how guys are."

"I know." Lina turned to Gary. "Move your car, asshole."

Joe grabbed Lina's car door. "I don't remember doing it. I swear."

Lina pulled the door free of his grip. "Take your family and friends away from here and stay away from my mother. Will you do that?"

Like with the thunderstorm twenty years before, Joe was about to cry.

"Get the hell out of my way."

Lina backed up and bumped Gary's car. Joe tried to get to the passenger door but Lina cut the wheel and

FUGUE

drove across the lawn, backing Joe off, chasing her mother
and step-father out of the way, and leaving them all behind.

CHAPTER NINETEEN

Harold gave Lina the nickel tour of his house. "I got lucky," he said. "The owners declared bankruptcy and the bank offered a short sale. I even bought their furniture. So I haven't done a thing to it."

And that, more than anything, captured what she remembered of Harold. He didn't seem to relish day-to-day living. And he never did anything unless it advanced his pursuit of becoming a doctor. *Harold* was all about becoming a doctor. So he had bought the house and everything in it because it was the simplest way to get a doctor's house.

But maybe that wasn't such a bad way to approach things.

"How do you clean it?" Lina asked.

"I hire a service."

"What do you even do here?"

"Not much. I'm at the hospital, or doing things elsewhere, so it doesn't even get dirty. Maybe a little dusty."

"So what did you spend on this place?"

"A few hundred thousand. My parents gave me the down payment as a graduation gift."

Lina nodded.

FUGUE

Harold was bothered by this and seemed uninterested in showing her the rest of the small mansion. "Well," Lina said. "You've just had such an easy life."

"Becoming a doctor is difficult."

Lina left it alone. She enjoyed plenty of advantages, herself, once her mother married an orthodontist. Had she played her cards right, her name would be on the deed of this house. Not that she wanted her name on the deed.

At least she didn't think she wanted her name on the deed.

Lina had a suite on the second floor. She hadn't brought that many things with her but there was a full complement of robes, towels, and toiletries in the closet. Harold's parents often stayed there for several days at a time now that they had moved their own residence to Fort Meyers.

She hadn't decided how many days she'd be here. The first priority was to get away from her parents, and Joe, and Joe's cast of crazies. She had thought little beyond that but it seemed time to get a job.

One room on the first floor was like a movie theater with a large screen against one wall and a popcorn machine on the other. Harold was set up in the middle, on a recliner, reading some kind of medical journal.

"Thanks again," Lina said. "I don't want to be a bother and you probably have plans. I'll go get something to eat and go to sleep after that."

"Wrong," Harold said. "I had plans but I changed them."

"You broke your date?"

"It's fine."

"Well what night is this, even? I've lost track of time."

"It's Friday."

129

"You broke your Friday night date. Now I feel bad."

"I changed my date. I'm having dinner with you. Will seven o'clock be all right?"

Lina was relieved to realize that Harold ordered dinner in. If he had become a doctor but also learned to cook this well, it wouldn't be fair. Maybe in later years, once he was established in his practice or something like that, and he could entertain hobbies like cooking.

Why the hell was she thinking about Harold's future? She wanted nothing with that. She was just here for a few days. Maybe a week, until she made her own arrangements and started her job search.

At least she'd get her computer set up and take at least one step back on the path she intended.

The path without Joe.

"You seem distracted," Harold said. "Is the food not good?"

"It's great. Thank you."

"Do you want to talk about something?"

"Not tonight. I need to get just a little distance between myself and my—"

There was a knock on the door.

The moment after Joe knocked, he realized he had not showered that day. He still smelled like Lake Erie, which was almost never a good thing. He may have showered the day before. Or not.

Harold opened the door and glared. "I don't want you here."

"I want to see—"

Harold closed the door.

Joe knocked on the door again.

FUGUE

Behind him, waiting in her car, Rhonda honked the horn.

Joe knocked again. He didn't want to even acknowledge that Rhonda was there. If she left, fine. He would not stop her.

But he would not leave without seeing Lina. So he knocked on the door again.

And then he pounded.

And he pounded once more.

Was it crazy, or stupid, or insensitive of him to want to see her? They were just a few minutes away from being married. They were just one drunken, stupid remark away from a lifetime of happiness.

How could she not want to give him that second chance?

The door opened and there was Lina, drinking a glass of water and looking at him.

"Hi," Joe said.

"I want you to leave. Now."

"I can't do that."

"I never want to see you again. Does that help?"

"No. Please, just let me—"

Lina threw water in his face. "Go. Now."

"Can I call you tomorrow?"

"No."

"Well, it was nice seeing you."

Lina closed the door.

It was nice seeing Lina. It confirmed his worst fear—that she would go to Harold. And she threw water at him but she didn't slap him or kick him in the nuts.

Maybe he would try to call her tomorrow.

In the car, Joe thought about Lina and what he might say to her the next day.

Rhonda drove. "Dad wants you to move out of the house. He's so pissed that he wanted me to tell you. I think he's afraid he'll punch you again."

"That's fine."

"What are your plans? Are you going to get a job and your own place to live?"

"Nope."

Rhonda stopped the car. It seemed she wasn't in the mood to not have a fight. "You can't do that," she said. "You should be pissed. If you don't stand up to Dad, then you're giving up."

"What do you care?"

"Not a whole lot but I don't want to see you become a total fucking waste. Don't just be a moron wandering the streets."

"Okay."

"So you know what you'll do?"

He was certain he knew what he would do but he also couldn't express it. There were no words for what he wanted to do—he thought in a series of colors in his mind, and the memory of a smell he couldn't name.

"The number three," he said.

"What is that?"

"Nothing. I smelled something, and I thought of the number three."

"Like a number one and a number two? Did you piss your pants and shit yourself?"

He touched his crotch. "Nope."

Rhonda shook her head and resumed driving. "What the fuck is going on with you?"

He shrugged. It seemed like a shrug was the best answer.

FUGUE

"Dad was so fucking pissed I thought his heart would explode."

"I think he was relieved when he punched me in the mouth."

"He enjoyed that," Rhonda said. "I think it frightened him how much he enjoyed punching you in the mouth."

"That's fine."

"So will you move out of the house?"

"Sure."

Rhonda stopped the car again, right in the lane. Cars honked, and Rhonda cussed back at them as they drove around her. "I think you're bullshitting me."

"How about if I get out now?"

"And do what, walk home?"

"Yes. To prove to you I'll move out of Dad's house, I'll not trouble you with driving me there, and will walk home."

"Do you have your phone with you?"

"No."

"Do you have any money?"

"No."

"Do you know where you'd go?"

"I'd walk to Gary's house."

"Oh fuck you," Rhonda said, and drove again. "That's twenty miles from here."

"Only ten."

"Fuck you."

"Can't say I didn't offer."

"That's just a pointless gesture," Rhonda said. "It'd be useless, wouldn't help you, and I guarantee you'd end up wandering the streets like a moron. This would be that moment and I don't want you to blame me for becoming that homeless idiot. If you want to do that, do it to your-self."

"Maybe I will," Joe said. He knew it was a stupid thing to say but he just wanted to piss off his sister.

The next day, Lina moved the desk in her bedroom to a spot where it caught the light in the afternoon. The day after that she set the laptop up in the other bedroom that shared this bathroom, and spread out some of her papers, binders and books on that bed. This was a more workable approach and she referred to that bedroom as the office.

But she didn't say that to Harold. He asked both days if she needed anything. She didn't.

On the third day she asked for help and they brought a load of her things over from her mother's garage. These were the recent accumulations of school work, papers, and studies. Most of this went into Harold's trash.

What she set aside with extra care were her journals and diaries. Almost all of them were leather-bound but even the cardboard journals were Moleskines, and she lined the whole lot of them in chronological order near the pillow on the bed.

This from January 14 of the first diary: "Sat next to K. In choir but only talked to him once. I thought he smelled nice."

This from November 10 of the freshman year in col-lege: "Hungover until 2pm and then had to study. Sucked."

Scattered throughout that trove were memories she couldn't recall and it had nothing to do with cracking her skull on the floor of the church at her wedding. There were things she did not remember that she couldn't blame

FUGUE

on Joe, who, she realized, she had not thought about since that first day when he knocked on the door.

It was surprising he hadn't returned that same night, or the next morning, but maybe he'd gotten the message.

Another load from her mother's garage cleared out all of her college career. Two text books were worth keeping but she put them up for sale on Amazon, anyway. Some of the gadgets and furniture went on Craigslist. A lot of the clothes went to Plato's Closet.

And the things that Plato's refused she left at Goodwill. If she was going to start her life over, she damn well would do it in a new wardrobe.

The day after completing all of that, Lina realized she was bored and so she scrolled through all of her Dropbox, Evernote, and Simplenote accounts. These were used as tools to get through school she no longer needed. But she found a few tidbits scattered around about things she'd learned that sounded like something interesting she might want to pursue after college.

Well here she was after college and she owed it to herself to find all those tidbits.

One file had a list of companies she might like to work for.

Several notes mentioned a topic that might make an interesting career.

She had tagged over fifty websites as "potential employers".

It took the better part of two days *in the office* but she created a master list of jobs, companies, and industries that might interest her.

She stored that master list back into a notebook on Evernote and focused her attention on wardrobe, making meticulous lists of stores with sales and fashion that'd be worthy of her investment.

The fashion plan was given a budget and then she created a spending schedule based on her savings (not a lot) and her available credit (lots). It was the height of summer but most stores were bringing in their fall lineups, which was fine. You had to start with a few foundational elements for the wardrobe and focus on interview-ready items such as suits. Get high-quality white, bone, and cream blouses. Let the accessories bring the color. Don't forget about a nice attache.

One professor, Susan, as she and Lina were on a first-name basis, at some point told Lina to let her know whenever Lina was ready to start a career and she'd offer advice. It was written, old school, on a note attached to a letter of reference Lina requested for an internship and the note was signed in ink. That offer sounded like such a good idea that Lina compiled a list of all her college professors, tracked down each email address, and sent them all a note asking for advice now that she had both a Bachelor and a Masters of Business Administration with a focus on finance.

This felt good, like she was doing something good for herself. Like the previous six years of college would not be wasted and would, in fact, take her somewhere she wanted to be.

On the next day, she continued her task of identifying potential employers.

She updated her resume and created cover letters for the top six firms. It was a textbook job search and she felt good about herself.

She even realized it had been a few days since she last tapped her fingers.

FUGUE

Once Lina decided there wasn't anything else to do that might improve her cover letters, she applied for the jobs. It was half an hour of tedium to visit the page, create a profile, and upload the cover letter and resume. Because of the wedding, she hadn't taken part in the interviews on campus. She couldn't recall why she thought that was a good idea. Maybe that was the last bit of her amnesia, or maybe she'd just been stupid in love with the idea of getting married.

The following evening, Harold was late getting home, and Lina prepared the meal. Nothing fancy—baked tilapia and a rice dish. But it turned out well.

"Thanks for cooking," Harold said. "I wasn't that hungry but I ate more because it was so good."

"You've been feeding me every night. I haven't thanked you enough for taking me in."

Harold refilled their wine glasses. "First, I have the room, so if we hated each other you could stay here for a year without us seeing each other. Second, I like you very much. I still love you. I don't mind saying that even if you haven't sorted out all of your feelings. Even if you moved out tomorrow, I wanted to let you know."

Lina injected no extra meaning into that conversation. Harold wasn't proclaiming his undying love for her. He was just supporting her, like a friend.

And his support was amazing. It was what she needed. But she also couldn't help noticing that she enjoyed their domestic situation.

Harold had a meal delivered each night and cleaned the dishes after.

In the morning, he made fruit and yogurt smoothies and saved one for Lina.

And the cleaning service that came in was instructed to do Lina's laundry.

He had to go out evenings—probably hospital business—and when he returned he checked in with her to see if she needed anything. There was no suggestion in his voice, either. He was a perfect gentleman and focused on her needs.

Why was he doing that?

The library at John Carroll was her home away from home. She spent more time there, studying in its main hall, than she did in all of her classes combined.

It was her habit, during school, to go to the library after each class and copy out her notes. This was her way to be sure that, if she got an answer wrong—ever—it wasn't because she hadn't looked at her notes.

Most of her friends took notes in class. That wasn't a big deal. And a few friends copied over their notes. Just a few. But none of them copied over their notes for every class.

Lina also had the best grades among her friend. Straight As, in fact. Including graduate school.

Sure, she had a few scares about her classes. But being here, in the library, was where she put those fears to rest. She rarely borrowed a book. She sat, copied notes, and thought about things.

Back in the dorm or in an apartment, her friends would have listened to music, watched television, or had a conversation while studying. Brittney was famous for that.

The only thing you could learn while studying with Brittney was which boy liked to get blow jobs. Poor,

FUGUE

sweet, Brittney. She took three years to realize that they all liked blow jobs.

The trick was figuring out which of the boys enjoyed returning the favor.

In the library, you didn't have to think about blow jobs unless you wanted to.

Joe always enjoyed returning the favor.

But all she had to do was prioritize her job interviews. She'd contacted a half dozen good companies—two in Cleveland, two in New York, and two in Chicago. Five of them had already contacted her via email and would arrange interviews soon. Maybe she should have chosen at least one in a warmer place, but she was going for a good business place to start her career, not a way to enjoy her life.

This visit to the library was like a victory lap. Enjoying the sights, sounds, and smells one last time before moving on.

As she left the library, the heat of the afternoon sun wrapped her up in its arms and so she sat on the cement steps and stretched her legs out. The trees and grass smelled like old times. She had sat right here on these steps dozens of times over the previous six years, feeling warm and relaxed. She'd also sat here in the fall, when the leaves swirled in the breeze and the air was crisp.

Maybe her favorite time was in the spring, when the breeze was cool but students were eager to enjoy it all and lounged on the wet grass just because they were happy to have survived another cold, miserable winter.

This was where she found Joe again, after having known each other as kids.

This place was one of the happiest places she'd known in her life. And now she was about to leave it for the last time.

She grabbed her phone and placed a call.

Harold sent a message to let Lina know that he'd be late but that he was looking forward to dinner with her.

She shopped for wine—in spite of Harold's collection—and bought a few things ready to prepare. She also roasted vegetables, set the table in the dining room, and lit candles.

"This is nice," Harold said. "Much better than eating in the kitchen."

"Have you eaten in the dining room?"

"I don't believe so. I've not had many guests. Just my parents."

The food seemed secondary to the wine, and Harold opened a second bottle. "You chose well," he said. "I'm impressed."

"Is that important to you? That your wife is someone who knows how to choose wine?"

"I suppose I want someone to spend my money."

"Then maybe you should marry Brittney."

"That's hilarious."

They drank more wine in front of the fireplace. It hadn't been used much, either, if at all.

"Do you mind?" Lina asked as she leaned against Harold.

He put his arm around her. It was like their first date, at the Jewish fraternity at college, when the music stopped, and people were scattered around the house making out or screwing around. Not that she felt like an

FUGUE

adult doing that with Harold but she felt like her mother was not part of the influence. And it wasn't like screwing Harold felt like a mistake back then.

Now, with the gas fire blazing and the second bottle of wine history, it seemed like the right thing to be there with Harold.

Harold turned her face up and kissed her.

So why should it be a mistake now?

Lina kissed him back.

Joe felt like they were there too late. He didn't want to go through with it.

"Horse shit," Gary said. "We shouldn't be doing this at all. What does it matter if we got here a little late."

Joe looked up and down the street. "Maybe I'm a little tired of being hassled by the cops."

"I promise to bail you out this time."

The subdivision was huge houses on over-sized lots. You could fit at least three of Joe's houses in the front yard and five more in back.

Joe checked the entranceway for cameras. "I also think their security systems will work well. I'm surprised there wasn't a guard at the entrance."

"What the fuck is your problem?" Gary asked. "I can't believe you're trying to puss-out now."

"Why do you even care? Do you want me to get Lina back, or do you want to see what happens when I go to her window."

"You'll break in, right?"

"No, I'm just going to tap on her window and ask her to elope."

"What the fuck good will that do?"

141

"What did you think I would do?"

"I thought you would punch that son of a bitch in the nose."

"And then what?'

"And then steal a television or something."

"I knew it," Joe said, and shoved Gary out of the way.

"Where the fuck are you going?"

"Back to the car."

They parked on a side street and had walked within a few houses of Harold's driveway. Gary cut across a lawn to get to the car first and locked the door.

"No way, man. Either you go in, or you walk home."

"Fine. I'll walk but we're through. Got that?"

"Great. I only liked you as a kid because I wanted to bang your sister."

Joe punched him. It came out of nowhere and he didn't even feel angry. And he didn't care to punch Gary again, even if Gary punched him back. It was all he wanted to do and now he would leave.

A car drove past them at high speed. Joe thought the car was familiar, and that the driver was even more so, but in the dark it's always hard to tell.

Gary punched Joe.

Joe was on the ground and his face hurt but he was more interested in the car that drove past because it pulled into Harold's driveway. "Who's that?"

"How the fuck should I know?"

"I think it's Brittney." Joe got up and walked back towards Harold's house. "What is she doing here?"

FUGUE

The front door opened and Lina grabbed at her clothes while Harold slipped on his boxer shorts and went into the hallway.

"Hello?" he said.

"Why are you here?" a woman's voice said. A *familiar* woman's voice—Brittney's.

There was a shawl on the chair and Lina grabbed it, slinging it across her chest just as Brittney walked into the room.

"Oh, fuck," Brittney said. "I knew it."

Lina tapped the fingers on her right hand with her thumb, one after the other—*index-middle-ring-pinkie, index-middle-ring-pinkie...*

Harold, like a true gentleman, got between them. "I was, uh— what are you doing here? Is everything all right?"

"Jesus, Harold," Brittney said. "Why aren't you wearing pants?"

All that Lina managed was her skirt before Brittney came into the family room, and now she was holding onto her underwear, bra, and blouse. "Hey Brittney."

"What the fuck is going on?"

"I think we'll ask Harold that question."

"You might have knocked, you know," Harold said. He crossed to the sofa and put on his trousers. "It's not what you think it is."

Brittney grabbed a vase from the table in the corner and smashed it against the wall, the wet flowers piled on the floor.

"How could you do this?"

Lina tapped her fingers, *index-middle-ring-pinkie...* "Brit, what the hell? We talked about this, about when you might talk to Harold."

"Screw that. You don't get to plan my love life."

"I wasn't going to plan it but you might have thought for a second about my feelings."

"Screw that too. You always had to have everything. Always had to be perfect. Well now you're a perfect whore, so congratulations."

Joe walked into the family room. It startled Brittney and confused Harold but it made sense to Lina. It seemed like the sort of thing he'd been doing for weeks and she was only surprised that she hadn't expected it of him.

"Don't talk to her like that," Joe said. "She's your friend. She wouldn't do anything to hurt you."

Brittney grabbed a book end and threw it at Joe's head. "Fuck you." She grabbed the books and threw them, chasing him out into the hall.

"Those are expensive," Harold said as he restrained Brittney but she slapped him away.

"Fuck you too."

Joe peeked into the room. "Listen, the front door was open so I—"

Harold came at Joe. "Get out of my house."

"I want to talk to Lina." Joe backed up as Harold pursued him into the hall but then Joe slipped back into the room, somehow evading Harold.

"Lina, I want to talk," Joe said. Lina watched his face as he realized—the blouse in Lina's hand and Harold's shirt on the floor—what had happened.

Lina tapped her fingers, *index-middle-ring-pinkie...* "Joe, you need to let me go." It was all so confusing, pitying Joe, kind of hating Brittney, and then wanting to see Mom. She wanted to see her mother. She *needed* to see her mother.

Harold grabbed Joe by the shoulder. "I want you—"

FUGUE

Joe turned and punched Harold in the nose. Joe stepped back and dropped his hands, not looking to fight more, almost inviting a beating.

But Harold was too busy staunching the blood gushing from his nose. Lina pressed Harold's shirt to his nose and walked him to the kitchen.

While he rinsed away the blood, she got him some ice. "I don't know if you meant to be an ass but this was bad."

"I didn't intend for it to be this bad."

"No? Well, congratulations. You shit on both of us at once."

Harold turned to her but Lina pressed the bag of ice into his face.

"Save it," she said. "I need to do a better job of covering up my tits before someone else arrives."

Lina returned to the other room and buttoned her blouse as she assessed the situation.

Joe sat in the chair, staring at the floor. He seemed comatose and maybe that was for the best at the moment.

Brittney leaned against the wall in the corner, sobbing and panting like a wounded animal.

"Brit, honey," Lina began. "I'm sorry. I didn't know."

"Well, fuck," Brittney said. "Neither did I."

"How long have you and Harold been dating?"

Brittney sat on the table she had just cleared off and leaned her back into the corner. He legs dangled above the floor. "Not even two weeks. It was right after you left me, and went back to your mother's. I thought you were staying there."

"Nope. I came here."

"*And* I thought you were pissed at me."

"Nope. I was feeling sorry for myself."

145

MICKEY HADICK

Brittney laughed but it wasn't because she was humored. "So how long have you and Harold, uh—"

Lina tapped her fingers, *index-middle-ring-pinkie…* "Just tonight. Kind of spur of the moment."

Brittney nodded. "I asked him if he wanted me to drop by, maybe hang here at his place, but he said it was too far out of the way for me. I thought he was being considerate. Tonight he said he was going back to the hospital but then I wondered." She looked at Harold returning and shook her head. "You seemed different. You ass."

"I was being considerate," Harold said as he lingered in the hallway, holding ice to his face. "I didn't intend for this to happen. Not like this."

Joe roused himself and looked around. "Sorry I punched you. If you want to punch me back, go ahead."

"That won't be necessary," Harold said as he stepped away.

There was a knock on the door and then Harold escorted two policeman into the room.

"Someone want to explain what's happening?" one of the cops said.

Harold pointed at Joe. "This man assaulted me."

"That true, buddy?"

Joe shrugged. "Is punching him in the nose assault?"

"Yes it is."

"Then yes I did."

One cop stepped into the hall and motioned for Joe to join him there. As Joe walked out, he turned for one more look back at Lina.

She shrugged. What else was she supposed to do?

The trailing cop put a hand on Joe's shoulder and hustled him away before anything else could be said.

FUGUE

She was pissed but also a bit grateful for Joe's intrusion. It was confusing but not the most confusing thing at the moment.

Harold came back into the room and looked at each of them but said nothing.

Lina wanted to be angry. "Did you have to call the cops?"

"He came into my home uninvited and bloodied my face."

Brittney hopped off of the table and Lina flinched in reflex, wary that Brit might just go crazy.

Lina noticed that Brit wore the Italian high heels with the long toe but they didn't go with those shorts. The color was not right for her. She needed sheer stocking to make that shade of orange work and Brit never, ever listened to Lina's advice.

Brittney clenched her fist so tightly that her arm shook. Lina was reminded that Brittney's terrible posture allowed no garment to hang as intended.

"This sucks," Brittney said. "I'm going to go have a good cry." She left and Harold followed her outside.

Lina heard them talking but had no interest. She didn't want to know what Harold was thinking, or what he intended to do next.

She hurried to her room and packed her things. On her way out the front door, Harold was just coming in.

"Please don't go. I think we need to talk."

"I need to get away," Lina said. "I thought I was when I came here but not even I knew what I was doing."

CHAPTER TWENTY

The Pepper Pike police station was nicer than Shaker Heights' and that made sense. The new money outgrew the old money and moved next door to the newer, nicer, more expensive residence. The rich folk would want that reflected in everything so that all who visited would know it was better than any other place. But like in any neighborhood, all who visited were not welcome.

"One day this will all be a pile of rubble," Joe said.

"Is that a threat?" the cop asked. "Are you making a threat?"

"I mean like Rome. Once Rome was the mightiest city on earth and now it's just rubble."

"So you're not making a threat?"

"I'm saying in two thousand years, Pepper Pike will be a pile of rubble."

"I'll mention it to the judge at your arraignment."

The cop's desk was mahogany and Joe's chair had a leather, padded seat where Joe rested his ass. There was a metal ring built into the arm rest to attach the handcuff so that the wood finish was protected. Also, the chair was bolted to the floor, probably so that no one tried hitting a cop with a chair.

FUGUE

"I'll be out of here in less than twenty-four hours. The jail that can hold me hasn't been built."

"I will ask you a couple of questions," the cop said as he settled his bulk into the swivel chair behind the desk. He took out a pen and pointed it at Joe. "Will you answer the questions?"

The cop took down Joe's information and then offered him the telephone to make his one call. "I suggest you choose carefully and get yourself a good lawyer. If I have to deal with you for long, you may get hurt."

"Is that a threat?"

For his one phone call, Joe first thought of Gary. But Joe could not stop himself from calling his father, considering that his father was likely asleep and would be furious if only because of the ringing phone.

It rang ten times before his father answered.

"I'm in jail, Dad."

"Where at?"

"Pepper Pike, I think."

"What did you do?"

"I punched Harold."

"Yeah. What do you want me to do?"

"Nothing. I plan on breaking out so you don't have to worry about me."

"Don't be a wise-ass. Nobody likes a wise-ass."

"I guess I would like a hug. You know, Dad, you never hugged much. Are you not a hugger, or did you think it'd toughen me up to not have hugs."

"Are you stupid, kid, or just acting stupid?"

"Nope. Neither. How about you, Dad? But were you drinking tonight?"

"Just shut the hell up and go to sleep."

149

"Awww, that's what you used to say when I had trouble sleeping after Mom died."

"I'm hanging up. Don't call back."

"Good night Dad."

His father hung up.

"Oh no," Joe said as he set the phone down.

"Oh no what?" the cop asked.

"I forgot to tell my Dad I loved him."

Joe awoke in the cell with his head resting on his arm.

The officer opening the door took a step back and waited.

"What time is it?" Joe asked.

"Time for you to get the hell up off that cot."

His shoulder hurt from the odd angle but he felt sad. "Is my dad here?"

"You're going to your arraignment," the cop said.

"Does that mean I'll go to jail?"

"You're already in jail, numb nuts. We'll march your ass over to the courthouse where you will talk to a lawyer and then sit before the judge while your charges are read out. Now get the hell on your feet."

"I have to go to the bathroom."

The officer pointed at the steel commode in the cell. "Then you'd better hurry and shit."

Both of Joe's wrists were handcuffed to the leather belt strapped around his waist. "What if I have to scratch my nose?"

"You'll find out who your friends are."

Joe was second in the line, behind an older guy. The guy was taller than Joe, wider than Joe, and hairy—he was balding on top but hair ran down the back of his neck like

FUGUE

a carpet and flowed out of his shirts sleeves down the length of his arms. His eyes were puffy from lack of sleep.

Behind him was a blonde woman who twitched and looked around like a frightened, caged animal, which they were. Joe couldn't get much of a read on the other two lined up, and didn't much care.

They marched at a snail's pace along a hallway from the jail cells to the courts.

The court room was much friendlier than the jail. Carpeted floors, padded chairs, and natural lighting. The officer led Joe and the other prisoners to two rows of chairs behind a railing in the corner. In the opposite corner was the judge's bench. On the other side of the room were padded benches for observers.

"You sit here," the officer said. "When the judge enters, stand up."

Over the next several minutes, people came into the court room and sat on the padded benches. No one seemed happy or comfortable. Anxious seemed to be the word of the day. Joe kept looking for his father each time the door opened, and each time he told himself to look away. It doesn't matter if he comes. No one is coming and that's fine.

But it wasn't fine. As the crowd grew, Joe's nose itched more and more. It was is if he could feel the breeze from the swing of the door and each time the tickle grew worse.

Joe tried to extend his tongue far enough to scratch his nose but he couldn't get close.

"What are you doing?" the guy next to him asked. "You trying to weird me out?"

"My nose itches. It's driving me nuts."

"Rub it on my shoulder. Go ahead, don't be shy. Maybe you can return the favor."

Joe rubbed his nose on the big guy's shoulder.

"Okay, don't make a spectacle of it."

"Thank you."

"So what did you do?" the big, hairy guy asked.

"I punched a guy."

The hairy guy nodded. "Did you kill him?"

"No."

"Oh. Well, I can teach you how to kill with one punch."

"Great. Thanks."

Carl had still not arrived by the time the judge entered the courtroom and began the proceedings. Joe had no reason to expect Carl to come at all other than simple hope. But it wasn't as if he cared that much. He had decided that he'd been wrong all of his life and was angry at himself for having made such a mistake.

But he also decided that he'd been right all of his life in not caring. What bothered him was that he thought it mattered that everyone else cared and that it was his choice to not care. Now he understood that it didn't matter whether anyone cared. Nothing mattered, except that his nose itched.

Hairy, Joe's nose-scratching friend was first to be charged. It turned out he had hospitalized a man with a single punch. This wasn't the first time Hairy had appeared before this judge, who was pissed.

Hairy said nothing in his own defense and so the judge scheduled the trial and ordered the bailiff to return Hairy to jail.

FUGUE

As Hairy marched past the defendant's box, he turned to Joe and said, "Look me up inside."

The judge took the next manila folder off of the stack and read, "Josep Kryznk."

Joe was escorted to the defendant's table and stood next to his court-appointed attorney, a disheveled man who was balding and thick around the middle, whom he had met before entering the court.

The judge looked up from the folder and scowled. "You are accused of assault and battery. How do you plead?"

The attorney—Joe couldn't remember his name—answered "not guilty." But he also pitched an idea to the judge, citing a program for first offenders.

The judge confirmed this with the prosecuting attorney, who looked on from the other table with disinterest. The judge tapped his gavel and pointed it at Joe. "Do you agree to what the court has proposed?"

Joe looked around and shrugged. "I wasn't listening."

The judge adjusted his glasses and glared at Joe, anger beaming from his pupils. "Let me spell it out for you, Mr. Kryznk. In the eyes of this court, you are an alien intruder to a community under its jurisdiction. You stand accused of assaulting a resident under the protection of this court. You also have no means of support. Is all that correct?"

"Yes, your honor."

The judge eased back in his seat. "This court has every intention of protecting its residents and will pursue every legal act available to it. Given your lack of means, it is likely you will end up in one of our jails at the expense of our community. However, if you can find and keep a job for six weeks, and break no other laws within the State of

Ohio during that same period, the charges against you to-day will be set aside. Will you agree to this?"

Joe shrugged. "Sure, your honor, but I don't have a job. I'm a full-time student on leave from active studies."

The judge's glare intensified. "This was supposed to have been arranged before presenting to the court."

"It has been, your honor," the attorney said. "The client's family has offered to secure a position with an industrial concern."

The judge nodded. "We will postpone the matter of setting a court date. Mr. Kryznk will be confined to the county jail until such time that he posts bail of five hundred dollars or presents sufficient proof to the prosecuting attorney that a bona fide, full-time job has been secured."

Joe turned to his attorney. "How am I supposed to find a job?"

The judge tapped his gavel. "Is there some problem?"

"No, your honor," the attorney said. "My client's sister offered to make the arrangements."

Joe tried to think of the conversation with the attorney but he knew for a fact he hadn't paid attention.

"Please advise the court of this employment," the judge said.

"Working with the defendant's father in the salt mines."

The judge nodded. "Well, there you have it Mr. Kryznk. Are you going to take the job with your father in a salt mine or go to jail?"

Joe looked from the judge to his attorney but said nothing.

FUGUE

The judge tapped his gavel. "The court must have an answer. Do you want to spend time with your father or do you want to go to jail?"

"I'm thinking," Joe said. "I'm thinking."

CHAPTER TWENTY-ONE

The Inn was not so much an inn as it was a crappy motel that may have been a decent motel during the previous century but was by far the worst place Lina had spent a night since leaving Parma. And that included her visit with a friend in Akron.

She was upset, and didn't understand what to do. There seemed no way to explain what had been happening. She couldn't explain it to herself. How could every single person who mattered in her life betray her?

She didn't think she'd be able to sleep once she laid down on the bed. The pillow smelled of Lysol, the mattress sagged in the middle, and light from the motel sign seeped in from every corner of the window. Trucks roared past on the highway and the headlights of every car passing on the road cast a weird light on the walls of the room.

She stared at the ceiling cursing her life and those in it, Harold for his pompous betrayal, Brittney for her narcissism, and Joe for being Joe, the stray dog that scratches at the back door, begging to get in.

How could anyone sleep in this place?

Her mother's house was less than ten miles away but now she felt like she was on the surface of the moon, never to see home again.

FUGUE

A sense of calm washed over her body. If she were on the surface of the moon then maybe she'd be able to fall asleep in the crappy little motel room.

The morning sunlight flooded the room and Lina opened her eyes in surrender. The steady rumble of trucks on the highway throbbed in her head. Maybe she slept. It was hard to tell. She hadn't bothered to undress and only crawled beneath the comforter on the bed to conceal herself.

She didn't want to admit it but some of the anger was gone.

And she still didn't understand what to do.

Of all the betrayals, her mother's was perhaps the least offensive because her mother was doing what she always did—meddling under the banner of loving concern.

Lina fired up her laptop to see how the job search was progressing. To take the proverbial bull by the horns. To seize the day. To leave the past in the past.

She expected to see a message from one firm she contacted but the only email was from her mentor, Susan, her professor at John Carrol. The email said, "Please call me as soon as you get this."

Lina called and Susan said, "We may have to rethink your job search strategy."

"Why?"

"Have you been on the internet?" Susan asked.

"No."

"A video from your wedding has gone viral. You're something of a sensation but not in the good way."

"Oh God."

"It'll be okay but you may not want to look at it alone. Come to my office."

But Lina couldn't wait.

She opened the browser on her computer and searched for 'wedding video.' A shudder spread across her body when her own face appeared in a thumbnail image of the results, the first result listed.

The video was an edited version of half a dozen cell phone videos uploaded after the wedding.

It was set to music. The beginning of the ceremony, the discussion with Joe, and the escalation into argument and accusation—including her scream—synchronized and auto-tuned with the music. The song built to a crescendo of synthesized tones and her head bouncing off of the floor of the church was in perfect step with electronic drum beats.

It had well over one million views. She'd be famous but for all of the wrong reasons.

Lina seemed about to vomit, then reached for something to throw across the room, and grabbed her phone. As she cocked it back to throw, she heard Susan's voice on the line.

"Lina!" Susan said. "It may not be as bad as it appears."

"I'll never work again."

"That's not true."

"I can't even show my face in Cleveland ever again."

"No. Not at all."

Lina slammed the laptop closed and pushed it off of the bed. "This is terrible."

"It's not terrible," Susan said. "But stay indoors for a few days. Or weeks."

Lina needed to disappear.

FUGUE

She tapped her thumb against her fingers, *index-middle-ring-pinkie.*

Her father had disappeared. So why couldn't she?

CHAPTER TWENTY-TWO

Joe's father helped him in the locker room with his gear. To work in a salt mine was more complicated than Joe ever realized, and a lot more complicated than Joe was comfortable with. In fact, he hated it—the helmet, the goggles, the breathing apparatus, the padded jumpsuit, and the steel toe boots.

"Don't forget your gloves," his father said.

"I wouldn't want that. I spent all that money on a manicure."

"Is that a joke?"

"Yes, Dad. That's a joke."

"There's no joking around in the hole, got it? People die down there."

"Great. I'm looking forward to it."

Joe had to relieve himself one more time, and so they were delayed getting to the elevator.

"God damn it," Carl said. "It's your first day. You don't want to be late."

"I don't want to piss myself, either."

They were the only ones left in the locker room, the others having already changed into their gear and gotten into the line for the elevators.

The whole thing was ridiculous. He'd been taken on in an assistant position, which only existed so the company

FUGUE

wouldn't have to pay union wages to some employees. If he lasted—that is, if he didn't get killed in the hole—he might be eligible for one of the union jobs, like his father's. Until then, he'd be paid better than minimum wage but he also had to reimburse the company for all of the safety gear so his pay would be docked down to nothing for the first three weeks.

And he wasn't even paid for the training—three days in a classroom listening to an idiot. At least six years of the community college had prepared him for that.

There was still a line of men waiting for the elevator.

"See," Joe said. "We're not even late."

"The problem is that you don't know how to work."

"I've worked plenty."

"Helping on a golf course is not work."

"Oh, you noticed what I did?"

"That was play. Here, you can get killed in the hole."

"If you keep mentioning that, Dad, I might think you're planning something."

They rode the elevator deep into the earth with four other guys, each of them dressed in a jumpsuit, toting an oxygen tank on their back, and holding gloves and helmet in hand. Joe was certain it would be four minutes he would never forget.

"You ever work in a salt mine?" one guy said.

"No," Joe said. "But I've heard it's lovely."

"He's never even worked before," his father said. "Period."

"Good way to start," the guy said. "Try not to get killed."

"I hope I'm not bored to death on this elevator."

MICKEY HADICK

The guy said to Carl, "Friend of yours?"

"My son," Carl said. "He hates everyone."

"I don't hate everyone. Just myself."

The guy nodded. "After a few days in the hole, you'll hate everyone else, too."

The descent took what little joy the men had in their eyes and replaced it with grim boredom.

When the elevator doors opened, the four other men walked off as if they knew their purpose. Joe lingered to look around—not that he cared. He had never seen it before.

There were two other elevators and a series of small sheds for equipment all within a lattice of steel beams, lights strung along the framework in what would be a decorative fashion if they weren't half a mile down.

Carl led him to the last of the sheds where a man with a clipboard and a handheld radio waited. The man checked Joe's name on the clipboard and then handed him a broom. "You work Bed Seven. You keep sweeping, okay? When you get a pile, scoop it into something holding salt. Got it?"

Past the sheds, beyond the lattice of steel, was a large cavern about the size of the church where he'd almost been married. Lamps cast pools of light, leaving much of the cavern shrouded in darkness.

"This is it?" Joe asked.

"This is just the beginning. Over there are the conveyors to the surface. That passage leads to Bed Two, where there is another conveyor to the surface. Those other passages are each active beds and you must watch out for the cargo trains. People are struck often."

FUGUE

"It doesn't seem like a big place."

"We're below Lake Erie. How big do you want it?"

"How far below are we?"

"I don't know, and I don't care."

Carl led him to Bed Seven explaining along the way what the various warning lights meant. "Flashing orange means fire in the hole. Make sure you have your ear muffs on."

A cargo train drove past. It was a small, six-wheeled utility truck, not much more than a seat on top of an engine with a steering wheel. It dragged eight trailers hitched together, train-like, all of them filled with salt.

"Don't get in their way. If you get hit, you'd be better off dead because the driver will beat you without mercy."

"Why would he do that?"

"Teamsters. They're sanctioned for accidents but, down here, the accidents are never the driver's fault. So stay out of their way. You don't want to piss off a Teamster."

The sweeping was easy enough, except that it was never ending and he was deep in a dark, noisy hole in the ground. But why should he enjoy the outdoors? Why should he be happy? He'd spent his entire life making jokes and it hadn't made him happy.

During the break, he sat with his father in the largest of the sheds, which was the cafeteria. Inside were eight long tables with chairs. There were vending machines along one wall, and a television in the corner.

"You can go up," his father said, "if you need fresh air."

"Nope. I'm fine."

"How do you like it."

"I don't."

"Sounds about right."

MICKEY HADICK

There was no conversation or friendly banter in the cafeteria. The men ate their food, stared at the television, and then got up to go back to work.

"I'll see you in a few hours," Carl said.

Joe nodded and grabbed his broom.

The whistle blew and the lights blinked. It was time for lunch.

Joe was never the first guy to lunch break because he was the not a fast walker. Sweeping took him to far corners of the mine. It was always a long walk. The Teamsters never offered a ride in their little carts. He was not a Teamster.

The lunch room was no bargain, anyway. It was like a lunch room back in junior high and the union guys were the cool kids. They had cliques. The United Mine Workers sat together at one end of the shed and the Teamsters sat at the other. Even within their groups, you could tell the *blasters* from the *scoopers*, and the *trolleys* from the *conveyors*.

Joe could have sat with the other three *sweepers* but he didn't give a shit if he had anyone to sit with at lunch. Same as junior high.

Sometimes his father sat with the scoopers but occasionally he sat with Joe.

This day, Carl made a point of joining Joe. "I have to tell you something," Carl said as he sat down. "The Teamsters are angry with you."

"They don't like how I sweep?"

"You don't get out of the way fast enough. You're making them slow down."

"I don't care."

FUGUE

"They might run you down. They care less than you do."

"I don't care if they run me down. What does it matter?"

"It matters. You don't want to die, do you?"

"I don't want to spend the rest of my life down here but there's also no reason to spend time on the surface."

"What are you saying?"

Joe stood up and rattled his chair against the floor.

"Stop that," Carl said.

Joe shoved the chair into a union guy at the next table. "Tell the Teamsters that if they want to run me down, go ahead. Just make it count, you fucking pussies."

"I'm not a Teamster," the guy said. "So go fuck yourself."

Carl pulled Joe away and walked him out of the shed. "Get a grip, God damn it. Be a man."

"Maybe I should just go do the time in jail."

They walked to the other side of the cavern, near the latrines where the smell of chemicals was thick.

"I know what your problem is. You're sad because of the girl but you'll see how those feelings go away. You might meet someone else but, if not, it will be okay."

"Dad, I don't want advice on love from you."

"I was married for over ten years. You think it didn't hurt to lose your mother?"

"Listen to yourself. She was your *wife*. You lost your *wife*. I lost my mother but you lost your wife. You should have been distraught, at least a little, but you never even cried."

"Crying wouldn't have helped the situation."

"Jesus, Dad, it wasn't a situation. It was our life. Our family. You still don't seem to care. Did you ever care?"

165

MICKEY HADICK

"I cared. She was my wife."

"She used to cry, you know."

"She wasn't happy about dying."

"Before then. When you were at the bar, she'd sit with me or with Rhonda in our beds and she'd cry. She said she was helping us get to sleep but she was unhappy."

"Why would you tell me this?"

"Because I don't think you ever understood why she died."

"She got sick. It was cancer."

"Yeah but I think she died of a broken heart. She didn't care if she lived. She didn't care if we lost our mother because she was that sad."

"Now you're being childish," Carl said. "You're not being a man about things." Then he walked toward the latrines.

Joe thought it was important to tell his father what he believed but now he wasn't so sure. Some people can't understand physics, some can't use a computer, and his father might never understand love. It wasn't his fault. It was just too bad, was all. "Maybe you're right, Dad."

Carl turned to look. "What?"

"I'm just being silly. Don't worry about it. But I think she missed you."

Carl shook his head. "Go do your job."

Joe walked by himself down a long, narrow corridor connecting the main chamber to the old dig hole. The blasting and scooping was going on far away from there in the new dig hole. His mission was to sweep all the salt dust in the old dig hole into a pile.

FUGUE

It was a stupid mission but no stupider than any other part of his job. On his second day, he asked his foreman why they didn't have a machine sweeping up the dust. It turned out that during the last contract negotiation, management wanted to use a mechanized vacuum but both the Teamsters and United Mine Workers wanted the position classified with their union. The Teamsters claimed it was like driving a truck. United Mine Workers insisted gathering salt dust was a mining activity. They compromised on a non-union position of broom pusher.

Joe would walk two miles into an abandoned hole and spend four hours pushing a broom. That was his life.

He earned this. This was the life he deserved. Walking alone toward a hole in the ground half a mile beneath Lake Erie was his destiny.

The corridor went dark.

The string of lights along the ceiling had shut down. The lights flickered often, and occasionally turned off. No chamber was dark for long. But this seemed different.

Joe turned on his helmet light and continued to walk. He considered turning back but didn't want to seem anything less than a man among these other men. Besides, the lights would come on eventually. The helmet light helped but it was disorienting to place his foot down into the darkness before him. He could hear the crunch of his boots on the salt dust echo from all around on the tight walls and low ceiling.

He sensed his approach to the main chamber as the echo changed. There was no air movement because the ventilation went off with the lights but the pressure seemed to change. It felt cooler.

Joe stood still before going in. It was pitch black beyond the reach of his helmet light and his skin tingled. There was no way to know what existed in such darkness.

Step inside and wait for the lights to turn on. Count to one hundred and if they aren't on by then, go back to the main chamber. He could tell the other men he'd been in the old dig hole but it's impossible to sweep with just the helmet lamp. They would respect that. In fact, they'd blame management, and herald Joe the next day during lunch.

Joe took two steps into the old dig hole and counted. When he got to ten, he heard two footsteps approach from the left.

The first blow landed before Joe could move and knocked off his helmet. Another blow landed in his gut and took his breath. He was shoved hard and Joe tasted salt as his face slammed to the floor.

There were kicks to his ribs, a kick to the stomach as he tried to roll away, and another to his crotch.

Joe curled into a ball—his only defense—and then a boot stomped on the side of his neck.

He listened to the footsteps of his assailant hurry away down the corridor. When it was silent, he allowed himself to groan in pain. Then, at last, the lights returned, and Joe checked himself for damage.

Joe held an ice bag to his face with one hand and another ice bag to his crotch with the other. Neither one helped much but at least it was something to do.

He had been blind-sided with no idea what provoked the attack, not unlike what happened at the wedding. But what was it about himself that provoked these problems.

FUGUE

He needed to figure out how to win back Lina. If he left this job now, which was what he wanted to do, he'd have to work out something with the judge or live as a fugitive. Neither option seemed like something he could do well.

But maybe he could just figure out how to contact Lina, as she had not responded to any of his entreaties in the three weeks since he last saw her.

His father opened the door and stared across the infirmary at Joe. "What the hell happened?"

Joe explained as best he could.

"Who did you piss off?"

"You know me. Everybody?"

"Do you need to go to the hospital?"

Joe shook his head.

"Then go back down the hole. That's the best thing." Carl closed the door as he left.

An x-ray found a cracked rib. Joe wanted nothing more than to use this as an excuse to take a day off but he still could not reach Lina and decided that at least in the salt mine he was not tempted to check his messages. Pushing a broom was doing something.

But he was not sure how he'd continue if Lina never, ever, returned his calls. Maybe this was why men used to join the French Foreign Legion. So maybe he didn't have to stay in the salt mine but he could try his luck in the Merchant Marine, or maybe as a fire spotter in a forest.

The next week, a Teamster stopped his trolley beside Joe in corridor where he swept.

"Get in," the Teamster said.

Joe thought it might be another set up but he was losing hope about Lina, so what did it matter if they murdered him in the hole.

They drove down the corridor where Joe had been attacked. There were two Teamsters standing guard at the entrance to the chamber.

There was just one light on in the chamber. Under the light were two more Teamsters dressed in their yellow jumpsuits. They stood over a third man, a miner wearing a light blue jumpsuit with his ankles zip tied together. One Teamster pressed his boot into the miner's throat. The other pressed a broom handle with all his weight onto the man's ass, pinning his lower body to the salt floor.

The man on the floor of the chamber twitched and squirmed.

The Teamster driving the gurney pointed. This is the guy that jumped you. He bragged about it to the wrong guy at the bar this weekend."

"Okay," Joe said. "If you say so."

"We want you to know we're not all animals down here. We watch out for each other."

The Teamsters pulled the pinned man's jumpsuit down to his waist and took turns pissing on him. He hissed and squirmed in fury but the Teamsters knew how to apply pressure.

They then duct taped his legs and arms and dragged him out of the light.

Joe heard the man grunt as they kicked him in the ribs.

The Teamster who gave Joe the ride came back to Joe and placed his hand on Joe's shoulder. "You want to land one in his balls?" he asked?

FUGUE

Joe met the Teamster's gaze under the shadow of the hard hat. "No thanks. It'll just hurt my ribs."

"Fair enough."

CHAPTER TWENTY-THREE

Lina sub-let a furnished one-bedroom apartment in Fremont, near enough to the community college to be among students. But it was a ghost town in summer, and that suited Lina fine. With her laptop turned off and her phone powered down, she couldn't be tracked.

Her first urge had been to hide in Port Clinton among the crowds of summer, but the only available rooms were beyond her supply of cash. Driving aimlessly away from the shore, she had come upon the tiny campus of the quiet town.

She shopped for food in Marblehead, did her laundry in Port Clinton, and only rented movies in Fremont, hoping to minimize her exposure to the world. She walked for exercise but never the same route twice.

It was clearly paranoia, but that didn't mean no one was after her.

After a couple of weeks, when it seemed no one in the area connected her to the internet-famous wedding video, she allowed herself to think about searching for her father. Besides, she'd seen all the movies at the crappy little rental shop.

Lina started the search in the only location ever mentioned in the same breath as her father. There had been a day when Lina overheard her mother talking on the

FUGUE

phone with Wayne's mother, about how her lawyer would handle the divorce because her father was confined to a VA hospital near Sandusky.

She visited that VA hospital on a Tuesday morning, going no farther than the information desk, and learning that her father was not a resident. The receptionist explained that it was rare for veterans to stay longer than a few weeks unless they were disabled. But she might check the hospitals in Port Clinton or Toledo, as well, depending on his condition. Or he might live near any of those hospitals, receiving government benefits, and visiting the hospital for treatments.

"I'm sorry I can't give you any more information than that. He really could be living anywhere."

"Do you have any advice?"

"What was your father's problem, if you don't mind me asking?"

"He was a drunk."

The receptionist nodded. "Port Clinton has lots of bars and plenty of drunks."

Lina started, instead, at the library. An internet search came up empty, which she half expected. It was possible her father had done nothing at all online.

She checked the phone books for Port Clinton and all the surrounding cities but found no mention of Joseph Finnerty. Again, given his circumstances, it was not surprising that her father would have established nothing like a permanent home. He was most likely paying cash for a cheap double-wide, paying for utilities at a liquor store. A little like she was doing at the moment, leaving no trace of presence. But she was doing it to create distance with her past, whereas her father would do it to live with as few responsibilities as possible.

Lina found nothing and would have to search the city on foot. And she would have to ignore the real possibility he wasn't even in this area. He could just as easily be in Fremont, or Sandusky, or Toledo. It reminded her of the feeling of dread at starting her master's thesis; she had to start somewhere and deal with everything else later.

She decided Port Clinton was dreary. There was a main strip that ran along the shoreline of Lake Erie. Along the avenue on either side of the highway exit, fast food restaurants, franchise taverns, and cheap motels crowded both sides of the street.

Heading west, a public beach allowed a view of the water for two miles with parking across the street and then older homes set back from the road. Some of the homes had a smidgen of charm as if, a hundred years earlier, wealthy people might have passed their days and evenings contemplating the waves upon the water.

And then she came to the downtown district with several blocks of old-time Americana storefronts, a nineteenth century hotel made of sandstone, and a dozen more taverns. Along the shore, there was a wharf and a marina with a ferry to the islands and half a dozen charter fishing operations.

After that was a draw bridge over the Portage river. On the other side of the bridge was more of the same.

Lina parked along the street and stood on the Western side of the bridge, looking back at the city on her right and Lake Erie on her left. Speed boats, fishing boats, and pleasure cruisers made their way along the river towards the lake. Farther out on the water were at least twenty sailboats. Farthest out of all of them was an ore freighter making its way along the horizon.

FUGUE

So many people enjoying the sunshine, busying themselves on the water, passing time until they returned to land where they would eat and drink themselves to sleep. It might just be possible to enjoy yourself in a place like this if only you could allow it. But Lina felt too frustrated at the moment for that.

Port Clinton wasn't paradise but there was no more reason to hate it than there was to hate Cleveland.

What made her unhappy were the people there, those who made fun of her wedding video, which was everybody. What she wanted was Cleveland without the Clevelanders.

She turned herself around, picked out a tavern and went inside to begin her search for her father.

CHAPTER TWENTY-FOUR

When Joe's court-ordered service was complete, his father took him out to the Pearl Tavern to celebrate.

Joe sat next to Carl at the bar. On Joe's other side was Retired Nick. Pete, manning the bar, leaned against the counter, watching the evening news.

They'd had a few beers already, and now waited for burgers and fries to be set before them on the bar. The woman in the kitchen was cooking.

After Joe's mother died, his father had gotten in the habit of bringing home meals from the Pearl Tavern. Hamburgers one night, fish sandwiches the next, and chicken wings after that. When Joe and Rhonda complained, Carl would make spaghetti, or maybe bring home a pizza. That's how they got all their food groups in.

As far as Joe knew, it was the same woman that always cooked here, and she might have cooked as many meals for Joe as his own mother had cooked.

Ken the plumber came in and sat next to Carl. "How's the kid doing?"

"Doing fine," Carl said. "They like him down in the hole."

"How'd you do it, kid?" Ken asked.

FUGUE

Joe looked up from his beer. "I push a broom and keep my mouth shut."

"Good work." Ken raised his beer mug in a toast.

"Next time someone dies down in the hole," Carl said, "they might offer him a union position."

Joe raised his own beer glass in salute. "If I'm lucky, there will be a cave-in, and then I might make foreman."

Carl frowned. "It worked out for the best. It's good work down in the hole. Once you have a good job, then you can get married. Before that, you don't even have a pot to piss in."

Ken bought them each another round. "My father knew what was best for me, too."

"So what drew you to plumbing? Life time fascination with toilets?"

"Plumbing? I hate it. But that was my only choice. My father paid a man to get my journeyman's card from the union and then paid another man to take me on, kind of like an apprentice."

"I bet you didn't have to hope for someone to die to get full time work."

"Nope," Ken said. "Just lots of clogged toilets."

Joe knocked on the door and waited.

"You?" Pauline asked when she opened the door. "What do you want?" She wore a robe and slippers. Her hair was a mess and she looked every second of her age.

Joe knew how she felt. "Any word from Lina?"

Pauline shook her head as she closed the door.

Joe blocked the door with his foot. "Please. The police have nothing on Lina's whereabouts?"

Pauline pressed the door with her shoulder, but then heaved a sigh. "They keep saying she did it on purpose. That she doesn't want to see me—or you—anymore."

"Do you have any guess on where she might have gone?"

"You know the video is your fault, too. What were you thinking, bringing strippers to your own wedding?"

"I didn't *bring* them."

Pauline looked tired, like she was too tired to be angry. "That's what men always say."

"When did her father die?" Joe asked.

Pauline looked with furrowed brow at Joe. "He didn't die. At least not that I heard."

"I assumed he was dead."

"He spent a year in a county jail. Then he moved out to Port Clinton and got sick and moved into a V.A. hospital."

"Do you think Lina may have gone there to visit him?"

"What in the hell for?"

"To fish?"

"Fish. She never fished in her life."

"Maybe she just wants to see her father."

Pauline pulled her robe tight around her chest and crossed her arms. "If she spends time with her father then the hell with the both of them."

Joe arrived back at his house to find Carl watering the front lawn. The lawn was clover and dandelion surrounding large clumps of crab grass. Why the hell was his father so intent on watering a crappy lawn?

Joe climbed the front steps but his father cut the water and called to him.

FUGUE

"I'm proud of you," he said. "You completed your service. You work in the mine. I'm giving you this house."

Joe took a moment to process this. He shrugged. "Okay, but Rhonda will be pissed."

"I'll make it right with her."

"What's the catch?"

Carl offered the hose. "Water the lawn."

"Um, sure."

"This is no joke. If you want the house, you must water the lawn."

"Jesus, Dad. You're the only person who gives a fuck about this lawn."

Carl dropped the hose and stepped in front of Joe. "I was not the only one."

Joe leaned back and glanced at his father. "Who else gave one shit?"

"Your mother."

"Why the hell would she care about the lawn?"

"Because it is like combing your hair. If you have messy hair, people think less of you."

"You watered this crappy lawn all these years because you thought it would make Mom happy?"

"Yes."

Joe laughed. It was all just ridiculous enough that Joe couldn't stop laughing.

Carl, his eyes wide with fury, grabbed Joe by the shirt. "Stand up."

Joe pushed Carl's hand away. "It's a little late to make Mom happy. She died ten years ago."

Carl dragged Joe up by one arm and flung him into the middle of the lawn. "You don't want this house, it's fine. You don't want to water this lawn, it's fine. But you get out. Understand?"

"Fuck it, Dad. Keep your house and water the lawn and pretend you're doing something nice in the memory of Mom. But she'll still be dead and that won't make up for treating her like shit—"

Carl's fist landed square on Joe's chin and a flash bulb went off in front of Joe's eyes. Then his ass hit the ground.

"Get up."

Joe noticed a cloud passing in front of the sun. His jaw hurt like hell but he got up. "You treated Mom like shit, and you didn't care about me or—"

Joe doubled over, the wind knocked out of him with a punch to the gut. "You didn't care for me or Rhonda. And, for the record, you didn't do that great of a fucking job with this lawn either."

Carl landed his fist on Joe's nose.

The pain radiated across Joe's face to the back of his head and then down to his kidneys. Blood gushed out of his nose. He sucked some into his mouth as he gasped for breath and the metallic taste coated his tongue.

Carl pressed a cloth under Joe's nose and got him to sit down and lean his head back. "Pinch the bridge," he said.

Joe remembered the stripper, then. She had gotten right in his face after the lap dance. She was offering him anything he wanted but he wasn't interested. But that hurt her feelings and Joe tried to make it up to her.

It seemed odd to Joe to have that memory triggered by a beating but it gave him a glimmer of hope.

Joe got to his feet and hugged his father. "Thanks for trying. I know you did your best."

Carl placed his hands on Joe's shoulder. "How hard did I hit you?"

"It's not that, Dad. I'm fine. Never been better."

FUGUE

"Stop talking nonsense. You need to get cleaned up. It's time for work."

Joe shook his head. "Tell them I quit," Joe said. "And give the house to Rhonda. I have to go find Lina."

CHAPTER TWENTY-FIVE

Joe drove west through Port Clinton toward downtown. The first taverns were sports bars. Joe did not consider going into sports bars. There would be sports fishermen—the kind with expensive boats and loud mouths. Men who would complain about professional baseball players.

The main drag had a beach and then a set of docks. There was a ferry arriving from the island out on the lake. Past the ferry boat there were some larger boats, charters for fishing, who were also in for the day and the boat captains were hosing off their boat, or putting away the gear.

Joe parked the car and approached one of the fishing charter boats. The captain was coiling a hose on the dock and glanced at Joe but went about his business.

"Can I ask you a question?"

The captain, a guy in his fifties, wearing jeans and a T-shirt and with a big belly, looked at Joe. "Ask away."

"Where would you go for a drink around here?"

"Do you want to watch the game on a big TV while you drink?"

"No. I want to drink."

"Then go to Charlie's Place." He pointed at a row of stores and restaurants down the street.

"Thanks."

FUGUE

Charlie's Place was in the middle of the block, wedged between a restaurant and a souvenir shop. It was about twenty feet wide, and was dark and had a low ceiling. It was a smaller version of the Pearl Tavern.

Joe picked out his spot at the bar. There were two middle-aged men at one end watching the game on the small television against the far wall. The sound was turned all the way down. They were just watching the baseball game.

A few stools away from them sat another guy, also middle-aged, sunburned like a lobster and drinking draft beer.

Joe sat one stool away from the lobster and ordered a draft beer.

He took his time drinking it. If he learned one thing from his father, hurrying through your beer is a waste of beer.

Joe ordered a second beer.

Right around the middle of that second beer, the lobster guy finished the one he was drinking, ordered another, and an extra for Joe.

"Thanks."

"You can owe me."

"Deal."

The lobster guy took his time drinking his beer. When he finished, Joe offered to buy him another.

"No thanks. I think I might go home and either shit or fall asleep."

Joe nodded. "Let me ask you, do you ever see a guy named Finnerty in here?"

The lobster guy took another look at Joe. "What for?"

"I'm engaged to his daughter. He took off about ten years ago and we think he came up here. Want to invite him to the wedding."

"Does he like to fish?"

"He liked to drink."

The lobster guy nodded. "What's he look like."

Joe described him as best he could, mentioning the jail time, veteran status, and how he might have aged since then.

"I don't think so. But you might try Paddy's Pub, next street over."

"Thanks. I will."

The next afternoon, Joe visited Paddy's Pub. Like Charlie's Place, it was a tight space and stuffed between a restaurant and an abandoned insurance agency. There were windows by the entrance but it got darker as you moved toward the back. There was also a television on the far wall but it was turned off. Nothing worth watching at this time of day, anyway.

There was just an older couple at a table near the front. They were drinking and not talking, and didn't seem interested in Joe as he made his way to the bar.

The bartender brought Joe his beer and then returned to the newspaper he'd been reading.

After a second beer, Joe asked, "Any other bars like this?"

"Like what?"

"Quiet. Charming. And friendly."

"Maybe you'd prefer T.G.I. Fridays or Finley's, out by the highway?"

"No. I like it here."

FUGUE

The bartender crossed his arms to think. "There's a gear shop over the bridge, and next to that is Frank's. But on weekends it's bikers."

"You mean like Hell's Angels?"

"Pleasure cruisers. Most of them boat, but they got those Honda cruisers."

Joe nodded. That would not be a place to check for Finnerty.

Joe ate walleye at the Jolly Roger, then took a walk along the docks. If he didn't make any progress in a day or two, he'd take the ferry out to the island and continue the search. It was possible Finnerty might have seasonal work there and there was no shortage of booze on Put-In-Bay.

But what if the old bastard had found God and given up drinking? Joe's best hope was that Finnerty stayed committed to the drink, like a good drunk should, and had found himself a new place to while away the hours, earning just enough money to quiet his nerves in a public house and drinking the rest of his pay with his own stash of bottles at his own place.

Joe made his way back to Paddy's Pub. It was after five and, like at Charlie's, the day before, there were a few middle-aged men at one end of the bar and a couple more at tables where they ate sandwiches and chips with their beer.

Joe took a place at the bar and ordered a beer and set about drinking it. Then he had another. As he wondered whether to order a third, or maybe take a look at Frank's over the bridge, the lobster guy came in and sat at the bar two stools away from Joe.

"You want to buy me that beer?" he asked.

Joe ordered two more beers. When they were finished, he asked, "You want another?"

"There's a guy in Charlie's might be the guy you're looking for."

"Finnerty?"

"I don't know his name. He came in a while ago, and then I remembered he's there a lot. Thought I'd let you know."

CHAPTER TWENTY-SIX

Lina had checked all the taverns in town and those on the strip at least once, and was making a third round of visits. After three visits, with times varied and days cross-referenced, she wasn't sure she'd visit them a fourth time. It had been two weeks already and her cash was running low.

For her own good, she'd walked the city, expecting to see more people, notice more things and accomplish her goal quicker than just driving up and down the main strip. But walking the two miles back and forth and then over to her crappy little rented room, it was not as much fun as she hoped.

Like any city anywhere, the year-round residents had year-round jobs, with bills to pay, and problems to solve. They didn't have time to chat. In fact, that was one of the tells for people not from around here—visitors stood around on the sidewalk outside the gift shops and antique stores, deciding where to go next. The locals piled back into their car and drove off to live the rest of their life.

Lina turned the corner on her way to Charlie's place and bumped into someone on the sidewalk.

"I'm sorry," she said and tried to get past.

"Lina?"

It was Joe.

"Hey! Small world."

"What are you doing here?"

"Looking for you."

"Well don't." Lina stepped past him and continued down the street.

Joe followed. "Are you looking for your father?"

"Yes. Now please leave me alone."

Joe pulled alongside of her. "He was at Charlie's a little while ago. That's one street over."

Lina gaped at him. "You were looking for me and you bumped into my father?"

"No. I was looking for you but figured if I found him, I'd find you."

Lina tapped her fingers with her thumb, *index-middle-ring-pinkie.* "That makes no sense."

"No?"

"Take me there."

They walked in silence to the next street over. Lina figured that Joe wanted to chat but she refused to give him an opening.

At the door to Charlie's, she turned and said, "I'm going in alone."

"Okay."

It was a low-ceilinged dive. Her eyes needed a second to adjust. When they did, she was convinced there was no one who looked like her father.

"Is there someone in the men's restroom?" she asked the bartender.

He shrugged.

Lina walked to the back and knocked on the door. With no reply, she opened the door a crack. "Anybody home?"

It was empty.

FUGUE

Out on the street, she found Joe standing a few paces off from where he'd been before. "He wasn't in there."

Joe nodded. "Must have left."

Lina shoved him. "Why didn't you stay with him?"

"He didn't feel like talking."

"You talked to him?"

"I did. I had to be sure it was him."

"So what did he say?"

"Not much."

Lina shoved Joe again. "You fucking idiot. You talked to my long-lost father but gave up because he didn't feel like talking?"

Joe shrugged. "He didn't remember me."

"I don't care. What did he say about me?"

"I guess I forgot to ask."

Lina shoved him a third time and walked away.

She stopped two store fronts away and tapped her fingers, *index-middle-ring-pinkie*, as she turned around. "Did he say where he lives?"

Joe shook his head. "No but I think I can figure it out."

An hour later, they had crisscrossed the area but saw no signs of her father.

"You didn't figure out shit," Lina said.

"Sorry. Do you want to go get something to eat?"

She wouldn't fall for this one. "I'll take you back to your car."

"How about tomorrow? We could get breakfast and then resume the search."

"I hate you," Lina said.

"That's encouraging," Joe said.

"How is that encouraging?"

"It means you still have feelings for me."

Joe followed Lina back to her place. After she was in-side and had enough time to get settled, he knocked on her door. Joe had no idea what he should say to Lina. The truth seemed his only chance but it made no more sense to him than high school algebra. And he had failed high school algebra.

When she opened the door, Lina's eyes and mouth turned down in disappointment. "What do you want?"

"To talk to you."

She shook her head again but this time her face was full of pity. "I don't think we should."

"I want to be a part of your life. And I want to tell you something."

Lina stepped outside and sat on the steps. "I'll listen but then I want you to go away."

Joe stepped down so he could face her. "I remember what happened at the bachelor party."

Lina folded her arms and waited.

"I know I said I didn't remember inviting the stripper to the wedding but now I remember."

"It popped back in your head?"

"I was hoping if I pretended it didn't happen it might go away."

Lina stood up and opened her door. "If you were five years old that might be a fine explanation." Then Lina closed the door.

Joe knocked. "I was ashamed. And embarrassed. I don't know why I invited her but I knew it was dumb. It's just that Gary was fooling around with the stripper and laughing at me because I wouldn't do anything with mine. And then the other guys were laughing and I got nervous and I wanted her to like me and know I was getting mar-ried. That I wasn't like those other guys."

FUGUE

There was no sound from inside the apartment.

Joe rested his head against the door and hoped Lina heard him. "I'm sorry. I hope that helps you understand why I did such a dumb thing. I wish I never did it. I wish I never messed things up."

Lina opened the door and looked at Joe. But he couldn't tell what she was feeling.

"Can you forgive me?"

"No."

Joe backed away from the steps.

Lina motioned for him to stop. "But tomorrow I want you to help me find my father."

CHAPTER TWENTY-SEVEN

It was P.J.'s routine to work on the docks scrubbing, stowing, or swabbing as needed, then do his chores around the boarding house and reward himself with a visit to the bar. He drank his couple of drinks, scrounged dinner, and picked up beer on the way home.

And so each day passed.

Off season he helped out at the local taverns, scrubbing toilets, stocking shelves, and mopping floors. Even if they paid him with peanuts, he was happy to have the tasks.

If there was one thing he learned from his time in jail, it's that a routine was essential to pass the time. Without routine, every minute of every hour of every day was excruciating. Without routine, you are in hell.

When the kid showed up claiming to have known him from before, P.J. was wary of upsetting his routine.

The kid shut the hell up when it was time to drink so P.J. didn't bother to move away. A few words exchanged over a drink was a good thing.

The kid showed up again the next day and P.J. got worried. But the kid bought a round and didn't seem to expect the favor returned.

FUGUE

Kid or not, the day was like most so there was that. It was almost time to scrounge dinner. Best to eat someplace else so as not to encourage the kid.

"Do you ever wonder about your daughter?" the kid said.

"What?"

"Lina. She's my age, now. Grown up."

"I figured that."

"She's a great person. Do you ever wonder about her?"

P.J. swallowed hard. He drained his glass and then raised it to his lips again out of habit. "I don't think about that stuff."

The kid shoved money across the bar and motioned for the bartender.

P.J. waited for the kid to look, to show his stupid face and open his stupid mouth. Say something stupid, kid, and you'll lose teeth.

"I bet she'd like to meet you," the kid said. "It's just been a while, is all."

P.J. emptied the glass again. He let it settle in his stomach. "I'm just an old drunk. Why'd she want something like that?"

"She thinks you're her dad."

P.J. hurried out the back and headed for his shed. There'd be no dinner tonight. That's what you get for messing with routine.

A hungry belly would remind him of what happens when he strayed. If he did just that, went straight to the shed and finished his business, then maybe he could have one of the extra beers kept on the shelf for an emergency.

But only if he did what he was supposed to do.

The shed was his and his alone. There was a bed and a chair and a small table and two lamps. It was warm enough in winter and cool during the summer.

There were no bugs or mice that lived there. Just him.

If there were guests in the rooms above the carriage house they could use his bathroom but even then he could lock the door while he was in there and keep it locked until he was through.

He liked the shed just fine.

It was too early to settle into bed. He turned on the radio and found a game being broadcast. Not the Indians but the Mud Hens. It didn't matter who, just that there was. So he sat in his chair to listen. If he made it to the end of the game, he'd give himself one of the emergency beers. Then he could think about the night.

He started in on the beers before the game ended but that was to be expected. The game was boring. He couldn't just sit there.

But then there was a knock on the door and he knew it was his fault. He shouldn't have changed the routine.

It was the kid from the bar. "Did you fucking follow me?"

"Just a little," the kid said. "I talked to the proprietor and he explained about the situation."

P.J. looked at the main house but no one was out back. In the next yard over there was movement near the garage but nothing he could discern. "Well?"

The kid smiled. "How are you doing?"

"What the hell do you want?"

"Would you like to meet your daughter?"

"Fuck off."

P.J. closed the door and locked it.

FUGUE

There was a knock on the door. "I'm sorry," the kid said. "I didn't mean to upset you."

P.J. snapped off the radio so he could think up words to say. "Leave me alone," was all he came up with. And then, "Beat it."

He sat in the quiet as the light faded in the window. He didn't bother to turn on the lamp.

Then, several minutes later, there was another knock on the door. Nothing was said, and P.J. offered nothing either.

He heard a car door open and close and then a car start and drive away.

A few more minutes after that, P.J. opened the door a crack to peek out. He saw a forty-ounce bottle of beer on the cement in front of the shed.

P.J. peeked around the dark yard. Seeing no one, he grabbed the beer and went back to his chair inside.

The next day, his routine seemed all wrong. His chores at the house went slowly. He felt like he was being watched. No one who knew him, other than the proprietor, had ever seen him in the shed.

He visited the docks to wait for the charter boats to return and he felt like anyone walking past might speak to him. For years he had existed as a shadow, standing among others but having no presence. It had been a gift, and now that fucking kid ruined it with his intrusion.

When one boat returned, he expected to see the kid step off the deck like one of the sunburned, lazy shits with nothing better to do with their time.

"I'm going right back out again," the captain said, refusing P.J.'s offer to help clean. "Maybe this evening."

P.J. was grateful and went to the tavern instead.

Frankie's Tavern was a longer walk but P.J. wanted a little distance between himself and where he had last seen the kid. It was no worse than the other taverns and the booze was just a cheap. The day might turn out okay yet, if he could scrounge more food than the tuna sandwich he bought at the gas station on his way to the docks earlier.

"Hey Patrick. How are you?"

It was the kid. The fucking kid stood just inside the front door smiling like an imbecile.

P.J. turned back to his drink. All he wanted to do was to be left to himself and—

"Hi Dad."

He looked again. There was a young lady next to the kid. She was a beautiful woman and stared at him with no shame. She looked familiar. Maybe even a little like his wife.

"Lina?"

"Yes, Dad."

He shook his head.

Lina stepped closer. "I'm sorry to bother you but I wanted to see you again."

His stomach tightened and he gasped for breath.

Lina stepped closer still. "I'll go away if you want. I want to tell you what's going on with me and to see how you are doing."

His ears felt hot as he struggled to find words.

Lina sat on the bar stool next to him and looked right at him, so close that P.J. could smell how pretty she was. "Okay Dad? Is it okay if we talk?"

P.J. nodded. Then he felt tears in his eyes.

"I'm sorry, Dad," she said. "Am I upsetting you?"

He shrugged. He still didn't have the words for what he felt.

FUGUE

"What, Dad? What?!"

He nodded his head.

"What?" Lina asked. "I'm upsetting you?"

"Yes," P.J. said. "You're upsetting me."

"Well too bad. You upset me when I was just a little girl and then I didn't see you for fourteen fucking years."

P.J. slammed his fist on the bar. "Okay. I'm sorry."

"Good. Is that it?"

"What else do you want?"

Lina set her hand on the bar near his own hand. "I want you to talk," she said.

P.J. got up and moved away from the bar. "I can't."

Lina took a step toward him but P.J. didn't wait. He hurried into the toilet and locked the door.

There was no knocking. No calls for him to come out. He heard their whispered discussion before they left but he wasn't waiting for them to leave. P.J. just wanted to be alone.

He sat on the toilet with his pants up and waited.

Jail was ten years ago now. It felt like a thousand years, a million years, since he was happy. Or if not happy, at least hopeful.

Going in scared him to death. It was just a county lock up but he had never been much of a fighter and didn't think he could defend himself. The friends he had at the bar were worried. They urged him to run away. Anything would be better than jail.

Once he was inside, he realized they had been right. He should have run away.

It was boring. The guards treated you like shit. The other prisoners treated you like shit. And if someone got angry you had to fight them because not fighting was far worse. They'd treat you worse than a sick dog if you showed fear.

Better to at least have thrown a punch than to run from a fight. Take the beating and suffer. But the cowards were shown no mercy.

He was inside for two years but it may as well have been a life time. He lost his job and couldn't find another. The friends at the bar had nothing for him. Not even a place to stay, like he was a God damn leper.

P.J. thought getting out of town was for the best. Sure he wondered what had become of Lina but what was the point of being her father if he couldn't act like a father?

Shit, once Pauline moved to the other side of Cleveland, there was no chance of seeing Lina, anyway.

He opened the door and stepped into the bar. It was quiet but not empty.

His drink had been refilled. As he settled onto the bar stool, he noticed the guy—that kid—sitting at the other end of the bar.

P.J. drained his glass. "Well?" he said. "What do you want?"

"I have an idea," the kid said.

CHAPTER TWENTY-EIGHT

Lina drove her father toward Cedar Point. Traveling through Sandusky, there was nothing special to see. The houses and corner bars could be any neighborhood in Cleveland. And the smell of the lake was waiting each time the window was cracked open.

When she turned onto the causeway and the Ferris wheel, the Needle, and the towering roller coasters came into view, her heart raced. But they weren't there yet as the traffic to get into the amusement park was backed up along the two mile road. Nothing was moving. Lina, not sure this was the best way to get reacquainted with her father, tapped her fingers with her thumb, *index-middle-ring-pinkie.*

"You learned that from me, you know."

"Learned what?"

"Tapping your fingers."

Lina looked down at her hand. "So you do it too?"

"Not anymore. But I guess that was the only thing I taught you before things went to hell."

"I don't remember that."

He shrugged. "When I told you I did it to help me deal with your mother, you did it too. I guess it wasn't like teaching you how to play guitar or nothing."

"I was seven."

P.J. shrugged. "It helped me get through jail."

"You don't do it anymore?"

P.J. didn't respond.

Lina glanced over. "Dad?"

He stared out the windshield.

"Do you need a doctor?"

"Where are we going?"

"To Cedar Point. Joe said he told you."

He shook his head.

"Don't you want to do some daddy-daughter things? We don't have to ride a roller coaster, but maybe we could go on the Ferris wheel?"

P.J. opened the car door and got out.

"Dad!"

By the time Lina got out of traffic and turned the car around, there was no sign of her father. Crying as she drove, worried that she'd wreck the car and kill herself before she had time to talk to him again, she parked the first place she could and got out.

He couldn't have gone far but she was so confused she wasn't sure she'd recognize him. Was his shirt green or brown? Was he wearing jeans? Why hadn't she paid better attention. It was only the second time she'd seen her father in over ten years and she'd hardly looked at him.

Along the cross road was a resort. A water park, in fact, that was part of Cedar Point. There was no chance he'd go there.

Farther back along the main drag was a small tavern, and she headed there on foot.

The walk gave her a chance to catch her breath. Maybe he was mentally ill. Obviously, he had anxiety issues—who didn't these days. Maybe he had a serious disorder and was undergoing a psychotic break with reality.

FUGUE

Or maybe he hated amusement parks. Was Coasterphobia a thing?

Inside, the tavern was dark and dingy. Kind of like the Pearl Tavern, where she and Joe joined Carl a couple of times for drinks.

Sure enough, P.J. was at the bar, already with a whisky in his hand.

Lina sat next to him and motioned for a drink just like his.

P.J. drained his glass and motioned for another. "I don't want to talk."

"Okay, and you don't want to go to the amusement park either. Is there anything you want to do?"

He touched his refilled glass to hers and took a sip.

"Fine."

"I like things the way they are."

Lina nodded and sipped her drink. "How did you stop the finger tapping?"

P.J. shrugged. "I decided to not be so pissed off about shit anymore."

"That's it?"

"I guess that was it. I didn't know it would take care of that dumb little habit. But I was tired of being pissed off."

"A Zen-like solution."

CHAPTER TWENTY-NINE

Joe knocked on Lina's door.

"Go away," she called from inside. There was no mistaking that she was upset.

"I want to know if there's anything I can do."

Lina opened the door. Her eyes were puffy and her nose red. "You've done enough."

"I'm sorry. It didn't go well, obviously, and I wish that was different. I wish a couple of other things were different."

Lina took a breath and stepped outside of her room, closing the door behind her. "Thank you for finding him. I know it's not your fault."

"Do you want to talk about it?"

She shook her head, then seemed to think better of it. "He wanted to drink. That's all he wants to do."

"Oh. I see."

"I had a drink with him, but I can't drink all day, let alone the rest of my life."

"Did you tell him you want to have a relationship, you know, because he's your dad?"

She nodded. "He said we can't have relationships with all the people in our life, even if we love them. He said it doesn't work for everybody, no matter how hard you try."

"Seems a little harsh."

FUGUE

Lina looked him in the eye. "It made sense to me."

Joe felt his throat swell up. "My dad has a drinking problem, too, but I don't want to be like my dad."

Lina held his gaze. "I don't want to see you anymore. It's too hard. The wedding, the internet, my parents…"

"No, please—"

"I'm going to move on. Without you."

Joe couldn't speak. He wasn't sure he could breathe.

Lina slipped back inside the apartment and closed the door.

Joe heard the dead bolt snap shut.

A week later, Lina took the bus to downtown Cleveland and walked into the Terminal Tower. She entered the flow of pedestrians on their way into the building and kept a wary eye on those around her. But no one paid her any attention.

Lina stopped at the security desk to contact her appointment. The guard wrote down her name, looked her over, but had no other recognition. He picked up the phone and called the business office on her behalf.

It seemed as many people continued out of the concourse and onto the downtown streets as waited for the elevators in the Tower. They all had place to go, something to do. But they all stared down at the phone held in their hand as they walked.

If she were to strip naked and stand in the middle of the concourse, most people would see her boobs because one or two guys snapped a picture and posted it on Reddit, or wherever, and then the rest of the idiots would comment on the picture, saying, "I was just there but I didn't see her."

Lina's meeting was with some guy whose business was to help people remove embarrassing photos and videos from the internet. She expected a young, cocky kid dressed in a T-shirt and jeans. Instead, it was a balding, middle-aged man wearing a suit.

"Have you ever been in the Tower?" he asked as they rode the elevator up.

"No. I appreciate the opportunity. Lived here all my life but never stopped in."

"I got in with a great lease when they damn near had to give the space away. Cleveland has not always been the strongest magnet for business, if you know what I mean."

The office was small. Support beams crowded the floor and the ceilings felt low. But it had a nice view of downtown and the lake beyond.

In the outer office, there were three young people, two women and a man, busy at laptop computers.

Lina and the owner went into his office. "Your academic credentials are impressive. You said on the phone you have experience in this area, this unfair usage of video. You want to tell me about it?"

Lina explained how she had researched getting her own wedding video taken down from the various websites and her tenacious pursuit of the website operators to comply.

"It turns out a letter works for most sites, but some sites take nothing down, ever. You have to sue them."

"Well, if you take the job, you can keep chasing them down. But I always ask my clients, do you really want to keep pursuing it? Things are forgotten pretty quickly on the internet. You know, another disaster arrives. The newest flavor of the week. Would maybe it be better to forget about it?"

FUGUE

Gary helped Joe move into an apartment. Together, they carried the sofa through the front door and set it against the wall.

Joe stretched out on it.

"I helped you move," Gary said. "Now you owe me."

"You helped me carry a sofa," Joe said. "That doesn't count as helping me move."

"If that's all of your belongings then, technically, I helped you move."

"Fine. I owe you."

Gary sat down in the middle of the floor. "Here's what I want. Tomorrow you're going boating with me."

"What? No."

"Yes. Summer is pretty much over. We've done nothing fun since the wedding, except when you got arrested. I'm bored."

Joe shook his head. "I need to shop for this place."

"You can do that Monday."

"I start my job Monday. I'm not messing that up."

Gary crawled to the sofa. "This is not just boating, man. This boat has a cabin up front. And I got the two strippers."

Joe lifted his head. "What?"

"Yeah, man. Don't you want to go boating on the lake with two strippers?"

"No. I'm fine."

Gary stood up and leaned over him on the sofa. "They still feel bad about ruining your wedding. It's remarkable they even remember us. This is an invitation to bang them."

Joe shook his head. Gary was still his friend but this seemed not right. It seemed like running barefoot across a minefield. Worse, it seemed like running with scissors while barefoot across a minefield.

Gary paced across the room, his steps echoing off the bare walls. "This is a sure thing. I have never been more sure of a sure thing in my life. This is as sure as cracking open a beer and knowing all you have to do is pour it into your mouth to taste the beer. This is as sure as that feeling in your gut in the morning when you have to take a royal dump."

Joe studied Gary as he paced the room. "Nope."

"Are you still mooning over what's her name?"

"Lina."

"I know her name, numb-nuts. I'm just saying, she hasn't given you any signs of wanting to bang you, right?'

"She hasn't answered a call or a text."

"So what is your deal?"

Joe felt empty. He worked his entire life toward his one dream of marrying Lina but, instead, he pissed her off so much that she wiped him from her memory. She even slept with her old boyfriend to prove she didn't love Joe.

But how do you say that to Gary, who thrived on emptiness and filled his life with nothing?

"I guess I'm not in the mood for fun," Joe said.

Gary pulled a can of beer from his back pocket and opened it up. "Give me one good reason you shouldn't party on a boat on Lake Erie with strippers who will at least give you a hand job."

Joe closed his eyes and rolled over on the couch. "I can't have any fun."

FUGUE

Gary chugged the beer and tossed the empty into the corner. "Okay, dingle berry, explain why you can't have fun?'

"Because I don't deserve it."

CHAPTER THIRTY

"Have you been waiting long?" Brittney asked. She had arrived twelve minutes after their appointed time, but Lina let it slide. "Not at all."

"Great." Brittney set her shopping bags next to the table and ordered wine.

They were at the restaurant on the top floor of The May Company, the last department store to remain downtown, anchoring the mall inside the Terminal Tower. The hoped-for revitalization hadn't, and Lina agreed to the lunch only because it was convenient for herself. She would make peace with Brittney and then move on, like a self-imposed twelve-step program.

"How are the wedding plans coming along?"

Brittney waited until the wine was poured. "Great. It's so much fun. This will be the best year of my life. Now I understand why you didn't want my help with yours."

Lina smiled. "It seems you'll be able to do it right."

Brittney nodded and motioned for more wine. "Harold is so supportive. He's given me carte blanche."

"He likes to speak French."

Brittney frowned. "What's that supposed to mean?"

"Sorry. Nothing."

FUGUE

Brittney furrowed her brow as she stared at the women eating at the next table. She took a breath and smiled at Lina. "I'd like you to be part of the wedding."

"That's sweet, Brit, but I think I have to sit this one out."

Brittney made her pouty face. "How come?"

"The wedding video disaster. I'll be a distraction."

"But you'll still come?"

"Wouldn't miss it for the world."

Brittney smiled but Lina wasn't sure if Brittney was happy that she would attend the wedding, or because the waitress was pouring more wine. Lina didn't believe for a second that Brittney wanted her in the wedding party. There would be plenty of young ladies to stand on the altar, and Brittney would want to know Lina was in the back of the church to witness how gorgeous and skinny Brittney was on the day she married a doctor.

After ordering food and hearing about Brittney's purchases, Lina realized she had nothing she wanted to say. Brittney's hair was tinted, but the color was wrong and seemed like a wig for a Halloween costume. She grabbed bread to distract herself.

"So where are you working?" Brittney asked.

"An internet service firm downtown."

Brittney's eyes opened wide. "Oh, like a startup? Are there millionaires?"

"It's a mom and pop without the mom."

"What's it called?"

"You wouldn't recognize it. I don' think I'll be there long. He's nice, but, I don't know."

"So where are you living?"

"I'm house-sitting for a friend of one of my professors. It's nice, but I won't be there too long."

"Okay."

Lina took another piece of bread. Brittney's earrings were wrong for the outfit, too. Such a simple thing, but she never got it right.

"So are you going to tell me anything?"

She saw her mother come into the restaurant and the bread caught in Lina's throat. After the coughing fit subsided, she looked for her mother and realized it wasn't her after all. Just a woman around the same age frowning at the hostess.

"Sorry I'm not very good company," she said. "I don't know what's wrong with me. I mean I know, but I don't know what to do."

"How's Joe?"

Lina shrugged. She'd rather talk about her mother, and she hated talking about her mother.

"That's too bad. You two were good together."

Lina scoffed. "Brit, you used to make fun of my dating him. You hated Joe."

"Yeah," Brittney said. "But you were more fun when he was around."

Lina was adept at the work but uninspired. Yet her boss appreciated her efforts.

"I can tell you don't love this," he said. "I don't love it either."

"So why do you do it?"

"I like making money. Mind you, I don't love making money. If you ain't making money, well, life is tough. So I start these businesses, see what works, try to find something that sticks."

"None of them stick?"

FUGUE

"Only I stick. My willingness to show up. To keep working. To try something new. I see you have that. You're dutiful and perfunctory. I like that in a person."

"I hope you're not proposing marriage."

"See? You're funny too. These other kids I got here, they are like brain dead. They mess with their phones. They're on the social networks doing God knows what. But not you."

"I'm lying low."

"That's the only way to stay out of trouble these days. I don't tell these kids not to mess around with the online stuff because that'd be bad for business. I wanted you to know I notice this."

"Thanks, I guess."

Because it was just the four of them in the small office, they had taken a break from their work and gathered in the outer office. In the two months that Lina worked there, she had just gotten to know the names of the other workers there, both of them part-time employees who were students at the university down the road.

She'd been living in a nice condominium downtown, house sitting for her mentor's friend from John Carroll. It was an easy commute and allowed her to avoid direct contact with her mother.

Lina had written to her mother and had no intention of avoiding her much longer. She hadn't decided what she would do next. Because the third question her mother would ask was, "What do you plan on doing next?"

She didn't yet know. Part of her missed her friends and family, and part of her was still smarting from how things had gone. Lina was also feeling silly about still figuring out what to do.

She knew it would soon be time to move on. Shit or get off the pot, as her father used to say back when they all lived in the tiny, one-bathroom house in Parma.

This job was simple and stress-free. It gave her the satisfaction of helping people who had been shamed online. But she hadn't dealt with the fact that the man she loved at one time had done something stupid during their wedding and driven them apart with the consequences.

She avoided these topics with her boss and coworkers. They stuck to the weather and the traffic, and she indulged a few conversations about sports teams or bands playing around town.

Nothing solid would come of this, ever, and so she knew she'd have to move on. This was a job. Somewhere out there, maybe in the same building, was a career, a life, and a family of her own.

Despite knowing she needed to move on, she had only lackadaisically searched for a job. When she began the search, she'd gotten sidetracked each time verifying that her wedding video had not made a resurgence in popularity. The worst case scenario was being picked up by a meme generator or included in a gify library and, luckily, neither had come to pass. The music video had run its course and faded into the internet sunset.

She should have been more aggressive with the search but she'd recently been stalking Brittney's wedding plans. As part of her scrubbing effort, Lina created a pseudonym account on Facebook. Brittney, not surprisingly, left her account open to the world, so every announcement, photo, and utterance she made was available.

Lina felt no particular twang of jealousy, but a general malaise she attributed to her life going off the road and into the ditch. So who cared if Brittney had chosen peach

FUGUE

chiffon, above-the-knee dresses for her bridesmaids? Or that she couldn't decide between Hawaii and Costa Rica for her honeymoon.

But this day she found herself stalking Joe online.

On Facebook, he had posted nothing since the wedding. But two weeks ago, Gary posted a snide remark, "loser would rather nap on his couch than boat on the lake. lame."

Lina remembered the naps on Joe's couch, both as a little kid and when they first dated. That sofa was the one piece of furniture he refused to part with when she'd redecorated his house.

And she hadn't insisted on replacing it because she didn't want to get rid of it either. It was a hideous couch, but it was a wonderful security blanket. She felt herself smile. How nice that he'd kept it. And also nice that he disappointed Gary.

She Googled Joe. Rather, she Googled 'kryznk'. There were just a few hits, most in Cyrillic font. But one hit was from a company called New American Salt:

"Welcoming Joe Kryznk to our inside sales team."

Their address was Public Square. In fact, the office was in the Terminal Tower, same as her own employer.

Joe was at the food court before 11:30, having gotten into a routine of eating early for the freshest hamburger and being back at his desk to prepare his afternoon sales calls. He'd learned that people will take calls soon after they've eaten lunch because they don't want to do actual work. Also, their belly full, they were more generous with their salt order.

MICKEY HADICK

But he also enjoyed the food court before it became crowded. Being the only customer at the counter placing an order reminded him of the hamburger joint on the corner, when he and Lina went there in the summer, before everything went to hell.

He chose the same seat every day, near the railing overlooking the lower level of the mall.

There was better food and a better view outside, but Joe was fine with this.

The problem with eating early and by yourself is that your mind has time to ruminate on things. And Joe had more than his share of *ruminate-able* things.

Could he have done something else in Port Clinton to keep Lina speaking to him?

Was barging in at Harold's house the wisest choice?

Should he have complimented the stripper on her dancing skills rather than inviting her to his wedding?

That one utterance had utterly destroyed his wedding. Or, that *udderance* had *udderly* destroyed his wedding. *Note to self: don't tell that joke to Lina if she ever speaks to me again.*

He settled in and arranged his French fries from smallest to biggest. Starting with the smallest, he dipped it in his milkshake before popping it in his mouth.

"Hello Joe," Lina said.

Startled, Joe bumped the table in his hurry to stand up and the milkshake spilled onto the fries. "What are you doing here?"

Lina helped him arrange the wrapper to contain the milkshake, and together they poured it, fries included, back into the cup. "Were you eating the fries from little to big? Like when we were kids?"

Joe nodded.

FUGUE

Lina burst into laughter.

Joe's heart fluttered. He hadn't heard that laugh since before the wedding. How he missed it.

"May I join you?"

Lina sat across from him at the table with her own hamburger, shake, and fries. She studied him. "How did you find this job?"

"Did you hear I went to the salt mines for, you know, punching Harold in the nose? I looked up distributors and called around. I figured I could use my experience down in the hole as leverage. I got lucky."

Lina nodded. "You weren't stalking me, trying to work in the same building?"

"I had no idea." But Joe couldn't keep from smiling. "Your mother claimed ignorance, and Brittney wouldn't talk to me. She kept waving the restraining order in my face. If I'd known, I would have looked for a job in the same company."

Lina leaned back in her chair, gazing at Joe without wavering. "I have to admit, it's kind of nice to see you."

Joe took a deep breath. No time like the present. "Would you like to go out to dinner? Maybe see what's going on downtown?"

Lina moved forward in her seat, studying him again. "Yes," she said. "That sounds like fun."

EPILOGUE

They married the following spring in a small ceremony at City Hall. Lina didn't want to rush it to be certain Joe was who she thought he was. And she decided against a large wedding, the memory of Brittney's and Harold's extravagant wedding still too close and nauseating.

Lina sent a letter inviting her father to give her away but, when she heard nothing back, decided it was for the best. She was a big girl now, and could give herself away at her own wedding. They would check in on him and buy him a drink.

Pauline was unhappy there would be no reception, but agreed to keep her complaints to herself in exchange for being invited.

Rhonda served as Maid of Honor. Gary stood up for Joe. Along with Carl, they all went out to share a meal, and that was it.

Lina knew the hardest part lay before them. But she faced it with no misgivings about their decision, and no expectation about their life together beyond the need to work very hard to make themselves happy as they took care of each other as best they could.

And that's how Lina and Joe got married.

ABOUT THE AUTHOR

Mickey Hadick lives near Lansing, Michigan where he has worked on short stories, novels, screenplays, and books for the past couple of decades.

He was born in Cleveland but ended up in Michigan by way of Pennsylvania. But the mistake on the lake will forever hold a special place in his heart, especially the view of the downtown skyline from the State Road hill in Parma, the exhaust flames jetting out of the stacks over the industrial complex in the flats, and the St. Theodosius dome watching over Tremont.

Whenever possible, he's telling stories, telling jokes, or messing around with computers.

He lives with his wife, two children, and a cat or two.

If you enjoyed this story and would like to get in on deals for future books, join him at:

www.mickeyhadick.com.

ACKNOWLEDGMENTS

This story began as a screenplay developed in a workshop back in 2011. Something wasn't right and I consulted with Steve Kaplan, an expert on comedy, and he pointed out many opportunities, not the least of which was making it a story of deeper meaning for myself.

I also needed to be a much better storyteller to make that work, and workshops with Donald Maas and Corey Mandell greatly improved my abilities.

Feedback from readers of the 2016 version encouraged me to rewrite it twice more in 2017, and that's what you have just read.

Many thanks to my wife, Mary and my now-adult children who have lived with my writing efforts for many years now.

Thanks and gratitude to the following people who provided feedback or otherwise supported my efforts:

Brian Wallace	Brian O'Neill
Michelle Linn	David Kusumoto
Tom Matt	John Hutson
Shelly Willoughby	Rebecca Ortese
Brock Post	Beckey Worden
Elisabeth Anderson	Sean Sully
Deb Kapcia	Chris Tyler
Shannon Hilliard	Kate Cosgrove
Janelle Manolakaudis	Michael Reibsome

PARKSIDE BOOKS

Be sure to check out the other titles available at:

www.parksidebooks.net

The way to make sure you get in on deals and book giveaways is to join Mickey Hadick's newsletter at:

www.mickeyhadick.com/updates/

BOUNTY FOR ERRORS

Although Parkside Books goes to great lengths to fix all errors before we go to print, we're not perfect. If you see a problem, please notify us via email at:

support@parksidebooks.net

In gratitude, we'll replace this title or send you a discount code for any of our other books, as you prefer.

Made in the USA
Columbia, SC
11 February 2018